CYNTHIA HICKEY

Bridge to Safety
Misty Hollow, Book 8

Cynthia Hickey

Copyright © 2023 Cynthia Hickey
Published by: Winged Publications

This book is a work of fiction. Names, characters, places, and incidents are the product of the author's imagination and are used fictitiously. Any resemblance to actual events, locales, or persons, living or dead, is coincidental.

No part of this book may be copied or distributed without the author's consent.

All rights reserved.

ISBN-13: 978-1-959788-58-4

DEDICATION

To my readers, to my husband who supports me, and to God who keeps the story ideas coming.

Chapter One

Shiloh Sloan could not believe she'd accepted a teaching job in her hometown of Misty Hollow. After all that had happened to her in that town, and now she was moving back? Even worse, she'd be living in her childhood home. With both her parents deceased, the house had been left to her. She'd meant to sell it a while back but never got around to it.

She placed a pile of books in the box on the bed and sealed it with strong packing tape before glancing around the furnished rental she'd lived in for the last five years. Shiloh had been relatively happy here. With a shrug, she lifted the box and set it with the others in the front room. The packing crew should be arriving soon. Once her belongings were on the truck, minus her suitcase and precious things that could be broken, she'd be on her way.

With a plaintiff sigh, she plopped onto the sofa and buried her head in her hands. What if the principal of the school she worked for made a move on her? She'd put him in his place, hadn't she? So why not return to the mountains to the place she'd once run from? Answer—because she'd almost had a repeat of that fateful prom night and needed a place to go.

A knock at the door made her bolt to her feet. A peek out the window brought a sigh of relief when she saw the logo on the moving van. She opened the door and stepped back.

Not having a lot of things, the van was packed and on its way in less than an hour. Shiloh took one last stroll through the house, then headed out to her four-wheel-drive SUV. She pressed the garage door opener and backed out, then realized the opener belonged to the house.

With a huff, she climbed from the vehicle and put the controller in the mailbox. Since she'd left the keys on the counter and pulled the door locked behind her, she couldn't do much more.

She slid into her vehicle and drove north toward the Ozark Mountains. Would she be able to call Misty Hollow home again? Surely, things would've changed. What had happened did so fifteen years ago. Would the town's residents still treat her as a liar? As a girl from the wrong side of the tracks whom they said coerced the town's football hero? At the time, she'd been shunned. Even her parents had looked at her with suspicion. Just because she ran a little wild during her teen years didn't make her a liar.

Now, she'd be teaching the children of those who's shunned her. They'd see soon enough how wrong they'd been.

The closer she got to the mountains, the more nervous she grew. Her palms sweated, and she took turns removing them from the steering wheel and wiping them on her jeans. She'd been wrong to accept the teaching position.

Four hours later, Misty Mountain loomed in front

of her. Dark clouds seemed to glare at her from their post on the summit. Great. She'd arrive in the rain. Could the day get any worse?

The clouds released their burden. The rain fell hard, obscuring her vision despite turning the windshield wipers on high.

She ran over something in the road. The thump elicited a shriek from her lips. Then, the telling pull of the steering wheel. The SUV had a flat...in the rain.

Her heart rate increased as she pulled as far to the side of the road as possible without ending up in the ditch. Shiloh willed her heartrate to return to normal as the wind outside picked up. She'd have to go out into the storm and unpack the back of the vehicle, setting her things on the ground in a downpour. Gritting her teeth, she shoved the door open. Within seconds, she was drenched, her hair plastered to her face. The hatchback provided a bit of protection from the rain, but it didn't help her belongings. She unloaded the back of the vehicle and removed the jack and spare tire from the wheel well.

Chilly raindrops slipped down the collar of the tee shirt she wore, and she shuddered. Changing a tire while a vehicle sat on uneven ground didn't sound like the best course of action.

She bit the inside of her cheek and glanced up and down the road, hoping for headlights. Nothing, of course. She was on her own. Shiloh stepped from under the protection of the rear door and stared at the slant of the road. There was absolutely no way she could safely change the tire without tipping the vehicle into the ditch.

She returned the jack and spare wheel to their

places, then repacked the back before dripping water all over the driver's seat as she climbed in to wait for help. On a lonely mountain road, help could be a long time coming. Teeth chattering, she checked her cell phone. No service. She locked the doors, wrapped her arms around her chest, and closed her eyes.

A tap on the window jolted her awake.

A face stared at her through the window.

She screamed.

~

"Whoa." Rowan backed up, holding up his hands. "I'm here to help."

The poor woman looked about ready to jump out of her skin. Despite the wide eyes and damp hair, it wasn't hard for him to see how beautiful she was. Auburn hair, eyes the color of a summer sun, a smattering of freckles across her cheeks.

He motioned for her to lower the window. When she did, just enough to be able to hear him, he introduced himself. "I'm Rowan Reynolds. I can give you a ride to the mechanic. They'll tow your car for you."

"Can you call a mechanic? I don't have service."

"Neither do I on this road. There's no service until you reach town. That's another five miles of winding road." He stepped back in hopes of reassuring her that he meant her no harm.

The rain had stopped, but the sky looked ready to dump more, and he didn't relish getting wet. Come on, lady. "I guess I can drive into town and send a truck back. You'll be out here alone for a while."

She frowned, then rolled up the window. The door opened, and she slid out, clutching a large bag. "Will they tow it today? Should I get my things out of the back?"

He glanced at his truck. "We can put your things in the back of my truck and try to beat the next downpour to your place. After that, we can head to the mechanic."

Another frown, then a reluctant nod before she opened the back of her vehicle. "I appreciate your help." She started unloading, handing him the boxes to put in the back of his truck. "This one can't get any wetter. I'll hold it on my lap."

"I'll put as much in the backseat as I can. Your suitcase looks like it can withstand the rain." He smiled at the bright pink hard-shell suitcase.

She nodded and continued to hand him things from the back until she'd emptied the vehicle. "Done. Of all the days to move." She climbed into the front seat of his truck before he could open the door for her.

He chuckled and got in the driver's seat. "Where to?"

"Do you know the old Sloan place? It's on the other side of the bridge that spans the river."

"No, I'm new to Misty Hollow. In fact, I need to let work know I'm going to be late. I'll make the call quick."

"No worries. I'm sure the moving van is waiting for me, though."

He placed the call, then headed for the bridge over Little River. "Mind telling me your name?"

"Oh. Sorry. I'm Shiloh Sloan, the new fifth-grade teacher at Misty Hollow Elementary."

"Sloan? We must be headed to your place."

"I grew up here. You're taking me to my childhood home."

"Well, welcome back."

She shrugged and stared out the side window as the rain started again. "We'll see." For the rest of the drive, an uncomfortable silence prevailed. Shiloh looked as if she wanted to melt into the door. She couldn't get any further away from Rowan and remain in the truck. He had a strong suspicion she didn't trust men and her childhood in Misty Hollow hadn't been a pleasant one.

"When you cross the bridge, turn right."

Other than give directions, she didn't speak until they turned onto a mountain road packed with cars. He pulled in front of a small white house badly in need of paint. The porch roof sagged on one corner. The steps had rotted away to where they weren't safe to use.

The river ran about half a football field from the front of the house. Hooked to a steel pole was a rusty fourteen-foot V-hull boat. At least someone had covered the motor.

Rowan wasn't one to pass judgment, but the house didn't look fit to live in. The van had obviously come and gone if the boxes piled on the porch were any indication.

"Looks pretty much as I left it." Shiloh opened her door. "I'm glad to see my things arrived."

"Let me help you carry everything in." He climbed out and opened the back door of his truck.

The inside of the house wasn't much better. Old-fashioned furniture, an inch of dust on everything, outdated appliances, and faded wallpaper. He glanced at the ceiling. No evidence of leaks which was one positive.

"I know it isn't much, but it can be fixed up. At

least I have a roof over my head. I've two days to get it in shape before starting my job." She set a box on the dinette set that looked as if it came straight from the 1950s. Maybe it did.

"We'll need to make a stop at the grocery store after the mechanic's. We can do that while they're fixing your tire." He rolled in her suitcase.

"Right. I'd forgotten I'd need food." She turned the kitchen faucet on. "Good. I called a few days ago to get the water and electricity turned on." Glancing around the room, she nodded. "I'm ready to head into town now." Those amazing eyes of hers turned toward him. "I can't thank you enough, Mr. Reynolds."

"Rowan, please." He smiled. "We'll be seeing a lot of each other. This town isn't that big."

"I know. Remember, I grew up here. I know exactly how this town is. Lately, there's been a lot of crime."

"Happens in secluded places, I guess." Rowan had fallen in love with the town since arriving six months ago. He couldn't imagine what could happen to someone to make them dislike it so much. Why had she returned if she hated the place so much? He bit back the question before asking. Why she came back was none of his concern. Unless she was in trouble.

That would make her his concern.

CYNTHIA HICKEY

Chapter Two

Shiloh froze as a man in dark coveralls came out of the mechanic's garage and wiped his hands on a red rag. Her heart dropped to her knees, and she staggered back, stepping on Rowan's toes.

"Steady." His strong hands on her shoulders held her upright. "You okay?"

Unable to speak, she nodded. No, she wasn't all right. The man striding her way with a big grin on his face was none other than Duke Larson—the last person she ever wanted to see again. The very person who had turned the town against her. The man who had the world on his shoulders and big plans to leave Misty Hollow. But he hadn't left. Shiloh really hadn't expected to see him. She thought she'd only have to overcome the prejudice of the town residents.

"Shiloh Sloan, I never thought you'd ever step foot in Misty Hollow again. You're looking good." Soft around the middle and balding, Duke barely resembled the football star of high school.

Some of the fear she'd held for fifteen years slipped away. "I'm the new fifth-grade teacher."

"Shiloh had a flat about halfway up the mountain," Rowan said. "Can you tow her SUV here? We'll be doing some shopping and can return in about an hour. Is that enough time?"

"Sure. I'm not busy today, but I'm breaking for lunch. Give me two hours." He puffed out his chest. "Since I now own this place, I reckon I can do whatever I want." As he spoke, his gaze remained on her.

The creepy feeling returned. "Thank you." She couldn't get back to Rowan's truck fast enough. Thankfully, the rain had stopped, and she didn't look like a drowned rat.

In the cab of the truck, Rowan turned to face her. "What's going on? You looked at that man as if you'd seen a ghost."

"I'd rather not talk about it, but he's the reason I left this town." She clicked her seatbelt into place. "Groceries?"

"Okay, but I'm here if you need me. Want to grab some lunch first? Lucy's Diner is as good as home-cooked food."

Shiloh wasn't sure she could eat a bite after seeing Duke but agreed. She did need to eat, and she hadn't had anything but gas-station junk since heading out that morning.

Rowan pulled into the parking lot of a diner that looked as if it had come from the 1950s. They pulled into the last empty spot. "You're going to love this place. It's the center of Misty Hollow. Everyone pops in on a regular basis. No better way to meet the town's residents."

She put a hand to her head. Could it get any worse? "After the soaking I had, I'm not presentable enough for first impressions." There had always been a diner of some sorts here. When she was a child, they hadn't been able to afford to eat out, not even an inexpensive place.

"You look fine." Rowan smiled and exited the truck. He held the diner door open and ushered her inside.

A young woman in her early twenties greeted them. "Two?"

"Yes. A booth please." Rowan put his hand on Shiloh's back, removing it when she jerked.

She took a steadying breath and followed the hostess to a booth near the kitchen. Rowan stopped at a table. "Sheriff Westbrook, meet Shiloh Sloan, the new fifth-grade teacher."

A handsome man set down his coffee and stood, offering her his hand. "Pleased to meet you, ma'am. How'd you end up with this hooligan?"

"I had a flat on my way into town, and Rowan stopped. Duke Larson is going to tow the car and fix the flat."

"Good. Welcome to Misty Hollow." He resumed his seat. "You need anything at all, you come into the office. We'll take care of it."

"Thank—" She bit off the words as Duke entered the diner. It occurred to her that she would run into him on a regular basis.

Both Rowan and the sheriff followed her gaze, then glanced at each other. Something passed between the two men that she couldn't exactly fathom. She turned from the door and rushed to the booth the hostess had assigned them.

The sheriff and Rowan conversed for a minute, then Rowan joined her, sliding into the seat opposite her. "Today's special is potato soup. Lucy's soup is to die for and comes with a big hunk of bread."

"Sounds delicious." Shiloh forced a smile. If she stayed in her thoughts, he'd grow suspicious and start asking questions again. She remembered how nosy the residents of small towns were and didn't want to be the cause of gossip again.

A woman with dyed red hair approached them, an order pad in her hand. "Nice to see you, Rowan." Her gaze flicked to Shiloh.

He made the introductions. "I want the special, as always. Shiloh?"

"The same." Her face hurt from keeping a smile in place. What she needed was a quiet few days alone to adjust to being back. She glanced around the diner as she waited for her food. Mostly new faces. Good. She definitely wasn't ready to see anyone else she'd once known. Not yet.

~

Duke sat in the driver's seat of Shiloh's SUV and took a deep breath. He remembered that smell. She still wore the same perfume she did all those years ago. The scent that drove him insane with lust. He breathed again.

No, this one was different. More floral. His mind had played tricks on him.

Imagine his surprise when she pulled up to the garage. Wow. Shiloh had returned. Why? For a job? Or to face that fateful night fifteen years ago? He grinned. "She missed me."

He was certain of it. They'd been something special. Duke, the star quarterback, Shiloh the pretty girl from the wrong side of the bridge. They'd set tongues to wagging for sure. Until she'd opened her mouth and ruined it all.

His smile faded. Why was she really back?

His hold tightened on the steering wheel. Had she returned to ruin him? It wouldn't work. Just like it hadn't back then. The people of Misty Hollow loved him and his family. They wouldn't believe her lies now either.

Laughing, he exited the vehicle. She'd looked absolutely terrified at the garage and at the diner. Maybe her return was as innocent as she said. But, if not, he'd make her regret coming back.

Duke loaded the SUV onto the tow truck, then drove back to the garage. He couldn't wait to see her again when she came to claim her vehicle.

~

After following Shiloh around the local grocery store, Rowan drove her back to the mechanic. Chaperoning a beautiful woman around town hadn't been how he thought he'd spend his day off, but there were worse ways. He glanced at his watch. Time was running out. Only fifteen minutes remained before he had to pick up Rachel.

"I've taken up enough of your time." Shiloh slid from his truck. "Thank you. I'll transfer the groceries and head home."

"I'll help. We'll get done faster. Before you drive off, I want to give you my phone number. Phone or text me at any time." Rowan filled his arms with bags and stashed them in the back of the SUV sporting a new tire. He glanced around for Duke.

Shiloh seemed more relaxed with the man out of sight. What was the story between those two? He knew just the person to ask once he'd picked up Rachel. It wouldn't take long for him to learn all he needed to know about Shiloh.

Once Shiloh was headed home, he drove to the elementary school where his daughter paced the sidewalk. He reached over and shoved the passenger door open. "Sorry."

Looking as haughty as only an eight-year-old girl could, she climbed in. "You can't use work as an excuse today, Daddy."

"No, I was being a Good Samaritan."

Her eyes widened. "Okay. You're only a little late."

He chuckled. "Do you mind if we stop by Mrs. Mayfield's house? I'd like to ask her something."

"I don't mind as long as she has cookies."

"She always has cookies." June Mayfield, as he'd learned soon after arriving in town, knew everything there was to know about everyone.

"Of course, I have cookies," she said when Rachel asked. "You know where they are." She arched a brow in Rowan's direction. "I do believe your daddy wants to talk to me about something."

"You would be right." He kissed the top of Rachel's head. "Go on and get started on your homework. I won't be long."

"Head on into the living room, Rowan. I'll fetch some iced tea." Leaning on a cane, the old woman followed Rachel to the kitchen.

"Let me get it." He started to follow.

"No, sir. My kitchen, my rules. Sit." She waved a hand behind her. June returned without the cane and set a silver tray with a pitcher of tea, two cups, and a bowl of sugar on the coffee table. She poured them both cups, then sat in a floral-patterned chair across from him. "What brings you here today?"

"What can you tell me about the Sloan family?"

A furrow formed between her eyebrows. "The couple died, and their daughter, Shiloh, moved. Why?"

"Shiloh has returned and is as skittish as a new foal."

"Ah. Well, there's a story there, and it isn't a pretty one. Are you sure you want to hear it?" She sat back.

"Absolutely. She's returned to teach but doesn't seem happy to be here."

"I don't suppose she would." She plucked at a doily on the chair arm. "Richard Sloan was a drunk. His wife, Susan, was a mere mouse of a woman. Their only child, Shiloh, was left to run wild. She got into some trouble with drinking and running around with boys. They didn't have much money, just the shack they lived in. I suppose the girl returned to the house?"

At his nod, she continued. "To the town's dismay and his parents' horror, Duke Larson started hanging around with Shiloh."

"Why would anyone care?" He stirred sugar into his tea.

"He was the star quarterback, and she was a girl many thought was beneath him. This town had big plans for Duke." She shrugged. "Anyway, on the night of the senior prom, Shiloh was discovered staggering home by a deputy, beer on her breath, and her prom dress hanging off her shoulder. Her lip was split open, and her fancy hairdo had come undone. She told the deputy that Duke had raped her. No one believed her, not even her own mother. Shiloh left town the morning after her graduation."

He hadn't expected that story. "What do you believe?"

"Doesn't matter what I believe."

"It does to me."

"I think the poor girl was telling the truth. That Larson boy always did have a mean streak. Thought himself prince of the town. He could have any girl he wanted, but he wanted Shiloh. The poor thing never stood a chance. She see him yet?"

He explained about the flat tire. "Her face was as white as a sheet when he walked out of that garage."

"I guess she thought he'd have left town. He'd been offered a scholarship to college but blew his knee out playing football in a muddy field with his buddies before he could head off. She wouldn't have known that." June shook her head. "You watch out for her, Rowan. You watch her real close."

"Why?" His heart skipped a beat.

"Because Duke will take one of two options, neither good. One, he'll think she's come back to be with him, or two, he'll think she's come back to ruin him. His mean streak has only grown bigger as he's gotten older."

Chapter Three

Shiloh had bought a full supply of groceries but neglected to buy anything to help her clean up the dump she now called home. She placed a call to an electrician and a plumber to install a washer and drier on what had once been a screened-in porch, then morphed into her childhood bedroom .

List in hand, she marched to her car. Cleaning supplies, a hammer and nails, some paint—the list went on. She'd seen a mercantile in town yesterday when Rowan had been chaffeuring her around. Hopefully, it would have what she needed so she wouldn't have to drive off the mountain to the nearest large city.

She crossed the bridge over Little River, passing homes that had once been as shoddy as hers, but the younger generation had renovated them. People with better educations and more money. Well, she'd make her childhood home something to be proud of, given time.

She parked on Main Street, praying the owner of the mercantile wasn't the same Fred Murphy from when she was a child. The man had hated her family. Not that Shiloh could blame him. Her father had been driving the car that killed the man's son.

The man behind the counter was none other than Fred Murphy. She sighed, plastered on a smile, and approached the counter. Maybe he wouldn't recognize her.

The scowl on his face said he did. "What are you doing back?"

"Teaching." She handed him a list, knowing he'd take her money despite his feelings toward anyone with Sloan as their last name. "I'd like to purchase these, please, and to see a list of contractors if possible."

"Fixing up that ole shack?"

"Yes, sir." She kept the smile on her face.

"Hmmph. Still don't know why you'd return."

"To clear my name." The words slipped out before she could stop them. Was this the real reason she'd returned? To show this town they'd been wrong about her? The past had plagued her the last fifteen years, casting a pall over every aspect of her life. Fear of rejection had kept her from forming any lasting relationships.

The bell on the door behind her jingled.

Murphy grinned as he looked over her shoulder. "How ya doin', Duke?"

"It's a fine day, Fred. Weather's great. Work's good. Can't complain." He stepped up to the counter and gave Shiloh a sideways glance. "Hey, Shiloh."

"Duke." She stepped away and pretended to study the display of paint colors. The lemon yellow would brighten her kitchen. While the men talked instead of Murphy filling her order, she picked the paints she wanted for her house, then set them on the counter. "Two gallons of each, please, plus the pan and three rollers."

Murphy frowned. "You got the money for all this? It's going to add up."

"Yes." She gritted her teeth to prevent herself from saying something she'd regret. "I've been a teacher for more than ten years. I'm fine." And respectable and honest and not the dumb hillbilly girl everyone thought her to be.

"My apologies." Duke stepped aside. "Fred, you can take care of me once you've finished with Shiloh." He cast a smile her way. If not for the lecherous gleam in his eyes, she'd have fallen for his friendly ruse.

"If you're sure." Murphy started mixing her paint.

"How's the house?" Duke leaned his back against the counter as he studied her.

She could feel his eyes on her. "Fine. Needs work."

"I'm sure. Need any help?"

She narrowed her eyes. What was he up to? "No, thank you."

He shrugged. "Okay, but construction and renovation are what I do."

"I thought you were a mechanic."

"That, too." He winked. "I've got my fingers in all sorts of pies." He leaned close, his whisper sending shivers down her spine. "Remember? I once told you that I would own this town."

"What's taking you so long?" Shiloh crossed her arms, suddenly feeling dirty. She wanted nothing more than to flee the store but she knew she couldn't. Not without her things.

"Takes time." He jerked his head toward the door. "Nice car, good job, you've come up in the world, Shiloh Sloan."

"Thanks." She moved away and chose a pattern of contact paper to line her kitchen drawers, then added new knobs. Anything to keep from carrying on a conversation as if she and Duke were friends. They would never be friends.

"Here you go." Murphy bagged her purchases and added them up. "Duke, mind carrying these out to the...her car?"

"Sure thing." Duke grinned her way, grabbed the paint cans, and headed outside.

Murphy glared and wagged a finger in her face. "You stay away from that boy. Haven't you caused enough trouble around here? Don't dig it all up."

"You were wrong then, and you're wrong now." She hefted a sack into her arms and rushed outside.

Duke leaned against her car. "Want to have lunch?"

"No, thank you." She stashed the bag in the back of her SUV.

"Why not?"

She whipped around, face flushed. "Are you serious?! After what you did to me? Leave me alone." She went to open the driver's side door.

He grabbed her arm and spun her around to face him. "You going to start those lies again, Shiloh?" He slammed her against the car. "Because if you do, you'll regret it. Every. Single. Bit. This is my town. You'd best remember that." He pinched her cheeks together with one hand and forced a kiss on her. Then, with a hard pat on her cheek, he returned inside the store, whistling.

Her hand shook so hard she could barely open her door. She fell inside and locked the door before leaning her forehead on the steering wheel. Duke was going to be a problem. A big one.

She started the car and headed for the sheriff's office, the only place she might find help.

~

Rowan had just stepped into the reception area of the station when Shiloh burst in. Tears streaked her face. "What happened?"

"I need a restraining order." Her chest heaved.

"Come here." He motioned for her to follow him into the interview room. "Can I get you water or coffee?"

"No." She plopped into a chair and raised red eyes to his.

A small bruise the size of a finger had formed on both sides of her face. "Tell me what happened?" He clutched the pencil in his hand so hard it snapped in half.

Her eyes widened, and she shrank back. "Nothing." She started to stand.

"I'm sorry. Please." He set the broken pencil pieces aside. "Who put the bruises on your face?"

"Duke Larson forced a kiss on me and threatened me."

"Wait here." Rowan wanted to throttle the man. He left the room to retrieve a form for her to fill out and a pen. When he returned, he set them in front of her.

"A restraining order will take time, but filling this out will get things started."

She stared at the paper. "Who's the judge?"

"Hall."

She shoved the paper aside. "Never mind. I was in too much trouble as a teen. He'd never believe me."

She tilted her head. A suspicious glint shone from her eyes. "Why are you not surprised to hear about Duke?"

"I asked some questions." He sat back. "I'm sorry, but I could tell something about this town frightened you, yet you returned."

"Why didn't you tell me you were a deputy?" She crossed her arms.

Good. Her Fight was returning. "It didn't come up."

Planting her hands flat on the table, she pushed to her feet. "I'm sorry for wasting your time, but unless there's another judge in town, I'll pass."

"What about Duke?"

"I'll avoid him to the best of my ability."

"Where did this happen?"

"Outside the mercantile."

"Any witnesses?"

"Maybe Mr. Murphy, but he's already accused me of coming back to Misty Hollow to ruin Duke's life as I tried to years ago. He wouldn't be any help." She put a hand on the doorknob. "Thank you for listening."

"Shiloh, wait." He rushed after her, stopping her in the parking lot. "I'm serious. Call me if you ever need me, no matter how small or inconsequential. Okay?"

"Why do you care?"

"Because I'm a deputy, and I don't like to see a woman mistreated." Not to mention that he liked to think he was a decent human being.

"Deputy?" Doris Belwright, the receptionist, poked her head out the door. "Rachel is on the phone."

"Be right there." He studied the face of the woman in front of him. The bruises had darkened in the short time she'd been in the office. "Don't hesitate, please."

She nodded and got in her car.

He watched her drive from the parking lot before answering the phone. "Why didn't you call my cell phone, sweetie?"

"I don't want to be here today, Daddy. Alice won't make the cookies I want her to."

"You should be grateful she's making any at all. Sweetie, I love you, but don't call the main number anymore. Call my cell phone. I'll be home in time for supper."

"Pizza?"

"Sure." He hung up and knocked on the sheriff's door. "Got a minute?"

"Absolutely." He waved toward a chair.

Rowan explained about Shiloh wanting a restraining order. "Were you aware of the history between her and Duke?"

"No, I wasn't." He folded his arms on the top of his desk. "I'll have my wife pay her a friendly visit to make sure she's okay. Strike up a conversation. She's a good judge of character, my Karlie. Does Miss Sloan seem to trust you?"

"I'm not sure. The gal's hard to read. She has a shield that's hard to penetrate, but she was open about Duke."

"Leave work a little early today. Drive by her place and see if anything seems out of the ordinary. We'll keep an eye on her for a few days until things settle down."

"Thank you." Rowan stood. This week would be easy since he had the early shift, but next week he worked nights. It would be more difficult to check on her. The best he could do was drive by her place and make sure no other cars were nearby. He hoped her nod at calling him if she was in trouble wasn't just to placate him.

~

Her lips had tasted as sweet as they had fifteen years ago. Duke parked on the road far enough away not to draw suspicion.

He had a reason to be there but wanted to watch her for a while as she unloaded her car. The sun highlighted her amazing auburn hair with red. Those gorgeous eyes had widened when he'd squeezed her face between his fingers. The heat of her silky skin—skin he'd felt against him before—seemed to burn his fingers. The thirst for Shiloh had never been quenched. Now, it increased with seeing the pretty girl, now a beautiful woman. He wanted her more than ever.

With the last of her purchases in her hand, she reached up to close the hatchback and glanced toward the road. He didn't bother to slide down in the seat. There was no way she could tell who sat in the white van; nor could she see the logo.

He had a right to be here. Something she'd find out soon enough. As soon as her front door closed behind her, he turned the key in the ignition and drove forward.

Chapter Four

The doorbell rang a sad, slow tune as Shiloh set her purchases on the kitchen table. She either needed a new bell or new batteries. But the doorbell wasn't a high priority. Making the house more comfortable and not such an eyesore to the community was.

She opened the door. Her throat clogged up at the sight of Duke standing there with a toolbox.

"You called for a plumber and an electrician?" He grinned. "I'm the best." Duke pushed past her. "Where do you want me?"

Shiloh tried to swallow, tried to speak, but nothing. She simply pointed to the back room. When he headed that way, she sagged against the wall. Her nightmare had come true. Everywhere she went, there Duke would be. She'd made a mistake coming back to Misty Hollow.

"Do you already have the washer and dryer?" He called out from the back room. "Good idea turning your old bedroom into a laundry room. You there?"

With slow steps, she followed his voice. "They're coming today."

"Need help with anything else when I'm finished

here? I'm a jack-of-all-trades," he said, not glancing her way.

How could he have gone from threats to genial conversation? "No, thanks." She forced the words not to betray her fear. Never again would she show him fear.

This time he did glance over his shoulder. "Are you sure? There's a lot of work to be done around this old place. It's barely fit for anyone to live here. Needs a new roof. Some of the siding has dry rot, those stairs are a hazard. You need me, Shiloh." His tone hardened.

"I already have someone helping me." She whipped around and retrieved her phone from the table and sent Rowan a quick text to come quick and play along. He responded immediately that he'd be there right away.

"Who?"

Shiloh hadn't heard Duke come up behind her. "Rowan Reynolds." She turned to face him, not trusting him past a minute.

His features hardened; his eyes flashed. "The deputy? Why him?"

"He's my friend." She fought the urge to take a step back.

"The deputy won't have time, Shiloh." He shook his head, his harsh look replaced with one of pity as if she were simple-minded. "I'll be here tomorrow to fix the roof. It's supposed to rain in a few days."

"No."

"What do you mean, no?"

"You're a busy man. I'll handle it." She backed up until the table stopped her retreat.

"Look. You and me need an understanding…" He

glanced past her, a smile spreading across his face. "Good morning, Deputy."

"Duke." His gaze landed on Shiloh.

"Oh, you're still in uniform. I'm sorry." She quickly squeezed past Duke. "I wondered if you'd had time yet to order the new roof?"

"I planned on doing that when my shift ended." The corner of his mouth quirked. "Since I'm here, I might as well take a walk around the house, see what else I can add to my to-do list. I'm sure Duke can work on what he came for while you show me around."

"Sure, Deputy." Duke spun on his heel and marched to the soon-to-be laundry room.

Shiloh clutched Rowan's arm and dragged him outside. "I didn't know this town only had one plumber and electrician."

"It doesn't. You have bad luck." He crossed his arms. "What's going on?"

"He scares the spit out of me. He wants to do all the renovations around here. I panicked and said you were helping me. Thank you for coming."

"I spoke to the sheriff about your predicament."

"And?" She arched a brow.

"He told me to keep an eye on you." He smiled. "I guess helping around this place counts as that. If you don't mind me bringing Rachel when I get off work, we'll make a list of what needs to be done."

"That isn't necessary. As long as Duke realizes he isn't needed...or wanted, I'll be fine." She hoped.

"I really don't mind. Helping around here will teach Rachel some responsibility. See you at three-thirty? I'll bring a pizza."

What a strange thing to say about whoever Rachel

was. Wife, girlfriend, either one wouldn't be pleased with his comment.

"I don't think Duke will pressure you too much now. If he does, zip me another text. It won't take me long to get here." His gaze searched her face, then he slid into his car and drove away.

The uneasiness she'd felt returned. While he'd been here, she felt safe. Now, she didn't want to go back into the house. She smiled to see the truck carrying her new washer and dryer arrive. For a little while, she wouldn't be alone with Duke. When the delivery men who were also installing the appliances left, she'd make up an errand to do if Duke tried sticking around.

By three-thirty both Duke and the delivery men were gone. In the laundry room stood a shiny new washer and dryer. Shiloh should've probably painted the room before having the appliances installed, but she'd move them when she got around to painting.

"Shiloh?" Rowan called from the front porch.

She hurried to greet him, stopping at the sight of a little girl holding his hand.

"Shiloh, this is my daughter, Rachel."

Oh. She hadn't expected a child. So, he was married, then. She shouldn't have asked for his help. "I'm sorry. I didn't realize. Rowan, you're far too busy to help me. I'm sure your wife—"

"She's deceased." He frowned. "Is it a problem for Rachel to be here?"

"Not at all." She smiled. "I bet she can wield a mean paintbrush."

~

The surprise he'd seen at first drained from

Shiloh's face. At first, Rowan had thought he'd overstepped a boundary by bringing his daughter with him. "That's great. Mind if I use your restroom to change out of my uniform?" He nodded at the backpack in his free hand. "I always keep some regular clothes in my car."

"Not at all. Rachel can help me unpack the paint rollers."

"This isn't a very pretty house." Rachel wrinkled her nose.

Shiloh laughed. "No, it isn't, but it can be. Will you help me make it pretty?"

His daughter sighed. "Okay, but it won't be easy."

Chuckling, Rowan headed down the small hall toward a bathroom stuck in the fifties right down to the pink tub and toilet. He quickly changed into his street clothes and put his uniform in the car before joining the other two, pizza in hand. He set the box on the counter. "Do you plan on redoing the bathroom?"

Shiloh glanced up from where she was prying open a can of yellow paint. "Yes, why?"

"I have an old claw-foot tub in my shed that was left behind when I bought the place. Since I don't need it, could you use it? It would need resurfacing."

Her eyes lit up. "I'll buy it from you."

"No need. Just pay for the resurfacing. I'll be glad the lovely thing will have a home." He rolled up his sleeves. "I'm going to start on those front steps before you break a leg."

"But I didn't buy any wood."

"I picked some up on the way." He snatched the hammer and nails from the table and headed outside. The entire porch needed replacing, but it wasn't as bad as the steps.

Shiloh and his daughter were chattering away in the house, but he couldn't make out what they talked about. It provided a nice backdrop to his thoughts. How could he keep Shiloh safe? He couldn't be with her twenty-four-seven.

If Duke watched the house long enough, he'd pick out a pattern of when law enforcement drove by. From what Rowan had gathered from asking a few subtle questions around town earlier that day, a lot of people still thought a lot of Duke, but Rowan couldn't figure out why. To him, Duke Larson was a puffed-up rooster strutting his stuff when he had little to strut about. Except, the man did seem to be monopolizing the renovation market. Rowan would have to find someone else to do Shiloh's projects when he couldn't because of his work schedule. By the time he finished the stairs, the aroma of pizza drifted through the open door. He set aside the tools and entered the house, sniffing in appreciation. His stomach rumbled, reminding him of the time.

"I warmed it up," Shiloh said, handing him a paper plate. "I'm not a fan of cold pizza. There's soda in the fridge."

Rachel, mouth full of her supper, nodded. "I got a Coke."

"Great." He ruffled her hair. "You'll be up all night."

"No, I won't." She took a big swig from the can. "Bedtime is at eight-thirty. Alice never lets me have soda, even when there's no school the next day."

"Our babysitter," he replied at Shiloh's curious look. "Rachel is eight, in the third grade, and thinks she's thirteen."

"I see that." Shiloh's eyes sparkled. "Aren't you going to say anything about the wall behind you? Rachel painted it."

He turned and widened his eyes. Yellow streaked the wall next to the fridge, most of the dingy white showing through. It would definitely need another two coats. "Looks great." His gaze met Shiloh's amused one. At least she had a sense of humor. He'd have cringed and taken the brush away from his daughter.

"I'll redo it," he mouthed.

Shiloh shook her head. "I'm going to have her painting the wall behind the sofa after we eat. A lovely robin's-egg blue."

At least she hadn't picked dark colors. The lighter ones would be easy to paint over. "Do you want me in there or the kitchen?"

"Wherever you prefer. It all will get done eventually. Or, the two of you can head home. I hate that you're spending your Saturday afternoon doing my work."

"It's fun." Rachel punched the air. "I want to come back tomorrow."

"We'll see." Rowan grinned. "I've some chores to do myself at home, and you need to clean your room."

"But this is more fun."

"Seriously. Painting is relaxing to me." Shiloh tossed her empty plate in the trash. "I appreciate your help, but I can do this. Well, the painting and cleaning."

"I'll find you a contractor by the end of the day on Monday." He helped her clean up, then grabbed the can of blue paint and a roller. "Let's get this front room done."

By the time he'd finished and repainted the small section his daughter had done, Rachel was curled up on the sofa fast asleep.

Shiloh handed him a cup of coffee. "Thank you."

"Let's take this out and sit on your new steps. I didn't see any stain to treat them with."

"Forgot to buy some. I'll head into town early next week." She sat on the top step. "Rachel told me your wife got sick and died when Rachel was little."

He sat beside her. "Cancer, three years ago."

"I'm sorry."

"It was rough, but we moved here to make a fresh start." He cut a sideways glance at Shiloh's profile. She was the only woman to catch his interest since Rose. The first woman in three years, and she was in trouble. While he didn't mind helping her around the house, it couldn't become a permanent thing. He wouldn't put his daughter in danger, and a man like Duke could be very dangerous, indeed.

They sat in companionable silence as the sun lowered over the mountain, kissing the trees with crimson and gold.

With a sigh, he pushed to his feet. "I'd better put my daughter to bed."

Shiloh's eyes sparkled in the moonlight. "Thank you, again."

"Anytime." He flashed her a grin and went inside to retrieve his daughter.

As he drove home, he passed Duke locking up the garage. The man glared his way. When Rowan glanced in the rearview mirror, he was still staring after them.

Chapter Five

Sunday had passed peacefully, thank goodness. No Duke.

Rowan and Rachel had come by for a few hours in the afternoon to help paint, sort of. Whatever Rachel did needed redoing, which Rowan did after working on the front porch. Another weekend of painting indoors, and Shiloh could begin outside.

Monday morning, she stood in the doorway of her new schoolroom. A year of enriching young minds, minus the week she hadn't been there, stretched in front of her. Some of her students' parents would be people she'd gone to school with. How would they react at knowing she taught their children?

"Shiloh?"

She turned at her name and stared into the shocked face of someone she'd once been close to. "Hello, Susan." The former cheerleader had always been nice to her. If anyone had believed her story, it was Susan.

"I never guessed the Ms. Sloan who'd be teaching here would be you." She smiled. "How are you?"

"Good. You?"

"Engaged." She wiggled her fingers, flashing a diamond. "I also teach fifth grade. This will be like old times." Her smile faded. "I suppose you've seen Duke?"

"Unfortunately. I thought he had a scholarship and moved away." She stepped into her room, pulling a rolling box of supplies behind her.

"Blew out his knee." Susan followed her. She stopped in front of Shiloh and tilted her head. "Will you be okay?"

"I hope so. He's already bothering me. I shouldn't have come back." Feeling as if she'd said too much, she occupied herself with unpacking the box.

"I believed you," the other woman said softly. "Duke did the same to me. You were the only one brave enough to say anything."

"Really?" She stiffened. "The two of you dated for a long time. King and queen on the football field once upon a time." At least until Duke had turned his attention to Shiloh.

"We broke up because of him forcing himself on me after the homecoming dance. I told him if he didn't leave me alone, I'd tell everyone what he did." Her eyes shimmered. "The town would have believed me, too."

"Yes." Sweet, pretty, perfect Susan would've been believed.

She wrapped Shiloh in a hug before she could pull back. "Let's be friends. Leave the past where it belongs. You let me know if Duke gets to be too much. I'll sic the sheriff on him."

Shiloh laughed. "I bet you would." She relaxed and returned the hug. "I'll see you at lunch."

After unpacking, she headed to the playground where her students would be lined up and waiting. A little girl in front held a sign that read, *Ms. Sloan*.

"Hi, Shiloh." Rachel waved frantically as her class filed into the building.

Her teacher shook her head and put a finger to her lips. "It's Ms. Shiloh to you, young lady. At least at school." She tossed Shiloh a smile and ushered her students inside.

"Good morning, class. Follow me, please. I'm sure this will be an exciting year for all of us." Although she'd already had enough excitement since arriving in town considering the flat tire and Duke's forceful attention.

The class spent the first half of the day going over class rules and getting to know not only Shiloh, but each other. At lunchtime, she escorted them to the cafeteria, then took her lunch to the teacher's lounge.

Susan and one other woman sat at a table. Two other tables sat empty. Shiloh chose a seat across from the other fifth-grade teacher. "I'm Shiloh Sloan."

"I know who you are." She narrowed her eyes. "I'm Melinda Larson. Duke is my cousin."

Great. Rather than respond, Shiloh opened her lunch box and pulled out leftovers from the night before—Chinese food Rowan brought over.

"That's a long time ago, Melinda." Susan narrowed her eyes. "You know very well how Duke is. We women have to stick together."

Shiloh widened her eyes. If something had happened to Melinda, then why had she looked at Shiloh as if she had leprosy?

"Hello, ladies." The principal, Mr. White, joined them. "Hope you don't mind. The only teacher I don't know very well is Ms. Sloan."

"Not at all." Melinda smiled his way, batting her

lashes.

Shiloh arched a brow. The man wore a wedding ring for heaven's sake.

"How's the day going?" He smiled at Shiloh.

"Great. I have a wonderful class, although I know the honeymoon period won't last." She'd forgotten chopsticks, so she forked a mouthful of noodles into her mouth.

"The gossip mill says you grew up here?"

She nodded. "I'm renovating my childhood home. I live across the bridge." She waited for snarky remark. When none came, the chip on her shoulder shifted a bit. Maybe it wouldn't be as tough to work here as she'd thought.

"Well, I've heard you had it rough back then." The principal stood. "Welcome back. Your credentials are impeccable, and this school is lucky to have you." With a nod in her direction, he headed out of the room.

Shiloh ducked her head and smiled, pretending to focus on her lunch. The man had nicely, but firmly, put any gossip between the fifth-grade teachers to a halt. She figured he'd do the same with the other grades.

"Are you dating Deputy Reynolds?" Melinda bit into a lunchroom burger.

"No, we're just friends. I had a flat upon arriving in town, and he gave me a ride to the mechanic, the grocery store, then home."

"Heard he's been helping you with repairs."

"Yes." Good grief, it didn't take the gossip mill long at all.

"Also heard he's supposed to keep an eye on you because of Duke." She slapped her palms on the table and pushed to her feet. "My cousin is too smart to chase after the likes of you again." Nose in the air, she strode in the direction Mr. White had gone.

Shiloh shared a shocked look with Susan.

"Hurt people hurt others. There's a sad story there, I think," Susan said.

~

Rowan stopped at the home of Deacon Jones while cruising around town. There was no better contractor in town, and the man wouldn't make any unwelcome advances toward Shiloh. No, he'd be quick and efficient at working on any job she needed to be done.

The man sat on the porch, an unlit pipe between his teeth. "Sure, I'll help the girl. That old house can be fixed up real nice," he said after Rowan asked if he could help. "It's got good bones."

"I'll let her know. When can you stop by?"

"This evening after supper, so about six."

Rowan offered the man a handshake, which he reciprocated. "Thanks."

Back in his car, he drove to the school. As school-resource officer, he stopped by once a day whether they needed him or not, usually eating lunch with Rachel. He wasn't surprised to find Shiloh in the teacher's lounge. "How's it going?"

"Good." She grinned up at him. "You?"

"Here to have lunch with Rachel. How are you, Susan?"

"Can't complain, Deputy."

"Richard finally got on one knee, huh?" He flashed a grin, then headed for the cafeteria.

Shiloh fell into step beside him. "I have to pick up my students. They'll be finished with recess by now."

"No trouble today?"

"None."

"A man by the name of Deacon Jones will be stopping by around six for you to show him what needs fixing around the place. He's a solid, trustworthy man. Well-respected in town."

"Thank you." Outside, she headed toward the playground while he entered the cafeteria. The noise slapped him in the face. He never could understand why the students weren't made to keep the decibel level down to a healthy rate.

Rachel leaped up from her table and dashed toward him. "My teacher won't let me call Shiloh...Shiloh." Her brow furrowed.

"Are you supposed to be out of your seat?" He arched a brow.

"No, but no one will say anything because you're a deputy."

He cleared his throat. "Don't use me as an excuse to misbehave. Go sit down while I get my lunch. And, at school, you will call Shiloh, Ms. Sloan." He kissed the top of her head and went to purchase the day's offering.

The cafeteria ladies let him eat from the teacher's salad bar and heaped his plate with more than he could usually eat despite his protests. They also refused to let him pay, so he added money to a child's account that had a negative balance. A win-win for everyone. Doing his best not to go deaf from the noise, he sat next to Rachel and listened to her prattle on about this kid or that, the third-grade bully, and her class's pet guinea pig. "I can't wait until it's my turn to bring it home over the weekend."

Well, he could wait.

"Can you please tell my teacher to let me visit Shiloh's room at least twice a day?" Rachel patted his arm.

"No, I will not. She's working, and you're learning."

She gave a dramatic eye roll. "But I can help her, Daddy."

"Not this time." He finished eating, kissed his daughter's cheek, and went back to work. Rowan drove past the mechanic garage, relieved to see Duke in the bay working on a vehicle. He wouldn't take kindly to finding out about Deacon. Not if he truly thought Shiloh wanted him around, which any fool could see she didn't.

Duke glanced over and scowled.

Rowan tossed a wave and continued, not wanting to antagonize the man and make things worse. By three-thirty, he pulled into the car line at school to pick up his daughter on time. She reminded him every morning when he dropped her off that he'd forgotten her on the first day of school last week. He waved at Shiloh who was moving students to their proper places and smiled as Rachel climbed into the backseat. "I did good today, didn't I?"

"Let's see if the good behavior lasts." She hooked herself into her booster seat.

The words that came from his daughter's mouth kept him entertained on a daily basis. She reminded him of her mother so much it hurt. His gaze fell on Shiloh. But, there might be someone to fill the hole in his heart.

~

Duke watched from the safety of his van as Deacon Jones studied the roof of Shiloh's house, then continued around until he returned to the front.

She waited for him on the front porch that obviously someone had already been working on. The deputy, no doubt. Why hadn't she taken Duke seriously about letting him fix the house? He wouldn't charge her any money. After all, once the house was complete, and she realized they belonged together, he'd move in. Now, he had another problem to get rid of. He slammed his hand on the steering wheel, accidentally hitting the horn. Neither Shiloh nor Deacon glanced his way.

"Can I help you?" A young man carrying a bag of garbage approached his van.

"No, thank you."

"Are you lost?"

"Just taking a break."

"Okay." He didn't look convinced, but dropped the bag into the garbage can and returned to the house.

When Deacon finally left Shiloh's house, Duke turned the van around and followed the man home. As Deacon unlocked the door, Duke hurried to stand behind him. "I've a word to pick with you."

"Oh?" Deacon pivoted to face him, his eyes wide. "You shouldn't sneak up on a man, Duke. I could've been armed."

"You going to work on the Sloan house?"

"Yes. I'll start this weekend on the roof."

"That's a good idea." Duke crossed his arms.

"Why not? We're the only two contractors in town. There's plenty of work to go around, and you're busy with the garage."

"Not that busy. Shiloh is my girl. I'll fix the house." Heat rose up his neck.

"If she's your girl, then why hire someone else?"

He squared his shoulders. "I've always wondered about her story all those years ago. Maybe she was right."

Duke slammed the older man against the siding. "I'm warning you, old man. Turn down the job. She'll have no other option than me." If he didn't do as Duke ordered, he'd be very sorry.

Chapter Six

Shiloh's hand froze halfway to taking a premade salad from the refrigerator when footsteps sounded on the front porch. Her heart leaped into her throat at the sound of the doorbell, which still needed to be replaced. Its sad peal barely announced someone's arrival.

She closed the fridge and peered out the curtain, mentally adding a peephole to the growing to-do list.

A pretty, very pregnant red-haired woman stood on the porch. A large black dog sat at her feet. "Shiloh Sloan? It's Karlie Westbrook, the sheriff's wife."

When Shiloh opened the door, the woman thrust a box into her hands. "Welcome back to Misty Hollow." She smiled. "I've brought supper and dessert. I hope you like lasagna and cherry pie."

"I love both. Please, join me." Shiloh stepped aside, eyeing the dog. Maybe she should get one. At least she'd have some warning when someone approached the house.

"This is Shadow. She sticks to me like glue. I hope you don't mind that I brought her."

"Not at all. I'm actually thinking of getting a dog for myself."

"Excellent. The shelter has plenty that need good homes."

Since the lasagna was still warm, Shiloh set it in the center of the table and fetched plates along with the salad she'd planned on eating for supper. As they ate, Karlie filled Shiloh in on how she'd come to live in Misty Hollow.

"This town is a magnet for women in trouble." She flashed a grin before listing off the things that had happened in the last couple of years.

"Yet, you stayed."

"Of course. This town needs my husband." She shrugged. "Despite the dangers that have popped up, the people of this town are good. Usually, it's those from the outside that bring trouble to us."

Not this time. The trouble had already been here waiting for Shiloh's return. "Maybe a bigger sheriff's department would help keep the bad from coming here."

"Nah. As the daughter of a crime boss, I know firsthand that a town nestled deep in the mountains will always be a place people go to hide. What's unfortunate is that it happens more often now because we've been in the news so often. Some think this is an easy town to gain control of. it's not such a good place to hide after all, unless you want to stay in a secluded cabin somewhere. There are a lot of those." She glanced around the room. "This will be cute once it's done. I love the colors you chose."

"It's already a far cry from what it looked like when I grew up here."

"That's right. I've heard rumors about the return of Shiloh Sloan." She chuckled. "You should've seen the upturned noses when folks learned who my father is."

"Is?" Shiloh widened her eyes.

"He's in prison for life. A model citizen behind bars, it seems. Anyway, I've made a place for myself in this town now, and they've come to accept me. They will you, too." She wadded up her napkin. "Let me help you clean these dishes."

"No need, but thanks." Shiloh sat back in her chair and studied the face of the woman across from her. "You must be aware of why these people turn their noses up at me."

She nodded. "A drunk for a father, a mother who turned her back on you just as the town did. Well, I pegged Duke Larson for trouble as soon as I met him. The man gives me the creeps. Don't worry about him. This town has a great sheriff."

"I'm counting on it. Thank you for supper. Want to take the rest home with you?"

"No, you keep it for your lunch tomorrow." She took Shiloh's hands in hers. "You've got a friend in me if you want one. This town is lucky to have you. They'll see." She gave her a quick hug, then called for the dog to follow her outside.

Shiloh stepped onto the porch to watch them go, before returning inside and locking the door behind her. It definitely wouldn't hurt to have the sheriff's wife as a friend. At the very least, it would make her look better in the eyes of the town's residents.

Shiloh cleaned the dishes and stored the leftovers in the fridge before sitting down to work on the next day's lessons. She liked giving her students a couple of days to get to know each other and her before digging in too deep and handing out homework.

The sun had begun to set, casting the yard and house into shadows by the time she finished. The darkness never failed to cover her with loneliness. Yes, a dog would be a good thing for her. A companion in the night, and the best warning system she could have.

Plus, a big dog would also provide protection.

~

"Good afternoon." Rowan rolled down the car window while he waited in the pickup line for his daughter.

"Hey." Shiloh smiled, her purse hanging off one shoulder.

"You look pleased about something." He grinned.

"I'm going to the shelter to adopt a dog."

"Oh? Would you like company? Rachel loves that place. We go there on the weekend sometimes so she can play with the animals. I don't have a dog because of my work hours, so she'd be thrilled."

Shiloh seemed to hesitate for a moment, then nodded. "If you're sure it won't be an inconvenience."

"Absolutely not. Get in."

She slid into the front seat as Rachel skipped toward the car. She squealed in delight when he told her where they were going.

"I'm going to come over and play with your dog all the time," she informed Shiloh as she buckled herself into her booster seat.

Shiloh laughed. "You're very welcome to play with the dog. I'm sure he or she will need the exercise. Karlie Westbrook came over last night with her dog, and I realized how much company one would give me." Not to mention protection. She didn't have to say the real reason. He could guess.

"That's a great idea. Big or small?"

"Big." She didn't hesitate in her answer. "Is the shelter far?"

"About ten minutes. Do you mind if we stop by my place first so I can change?"

"Not at all."

At the house, he took Rachel's backpack inside and left the two in the car chattering about different types of dogs. His daughter would be begging for one of her own again, but with the way his schedule changed so often, he didn't think it fair to leave a dog alone for so long each day, not to mention Alice didn't like them.

Someday, maybe, he'd give Rachel a pet. For now, she'd have to be satisfied with Shiloh's. Rowan changed into jeans and a Tee-shirt before returning to the car. He smiled to hear Shiloh's laughter, the fear and tension gone from her face.

"We're going to call the dog, Peanut." Rachel gave a definitive nod.

"For a big dog?" He arched a brow at Shiloh.

"Your daughter is very persuasive."

"It has to be a brown dog, Daddy, because peanuts are brown."

"We'll do our best." He smiled in the rearview mirror. "I call you peanut. Who's going to come when I call? Won't you be confused?"

"No." She frowned. "I'm a girl, and this will be a dog."

"Wisely said." He pulled away from the house and drove to the shelter.

The barking of a choir of dogs reached his ears before he'd opened his car door. "There's the welcoming committee."

Inside, they entered the door under a sign that read large breeds. The cacophony of noise hurt his ears.

"This is not going to be easy." Shiloh peered into the cages. "They all look so sad."

"Why not check each cage, then go back to see which one seems right for you?"

Shiloh nodded, sadness coating her features. "I can discard any that say not good for children. I want a watchdog, not a beast." She stopped in front of a cage with the biggest, ugliest dog Rowan had ever seen. The animal's tail thumped the cement floor. "This one."

"Really?"

"Absolutely. She's the right color, too." The sign simply said *mixed breed*. "How do you feel about being called Peanut instead of Gracie?"

The dog continued to wag its tail.

"Let me go find someone to let her out. There's an area where prospective adoptees can spend some time with the animals." He returned to the front of the kennels.

"Oh, I'm so glad she's interested in that poor dog. She belonged to an old woman who passed away recently. She's a mix of mastiff, German shepherd, and Labrador, we think. Anyway," the girl said, "She's a real sweetheart. One of my favorites." She unlocked the dog's cage and slipped a leash around its neck.

Shiloh sat on the bench in the outdoor pen. Gracie, soon to be Peanut, laid her massive head on her knee. When Shiloh scratched the dog's ears, the dog closed her eyes and leaned into her.

Rowan smiled. The dog would be a good fit after all.

"My turn." Rachel wrapped her arms around the dog's neck.

Rowan prepared to leap forward when the dog's eyes snapped open in surprise. When no attack came, he relaxed. His daughter would be safe around Peanut. "So, do you have a new dog?"

"I sure do." She glanced up at the girl who stood near the gate. "What do I need to do?"

"Pay the fee. We supply you with the leash, but you'll need to purchase the other things."

"We can stop by the store on the way." Rowan held the gate open while Shiloh led out her new best friend.

Next stop…the nearest place to purchase what she needed. The mercantile. Leaving the dog in the car, Rowan followed Shiloh and his daughter into the store.

Fred seemed surprised to see the three of them together. "Deputy."

"Shiloh just adopted a dog. She's in need of supplies." He pierced the man with a sharp look. "I'm sure you can help her out."

"Sure, sure. Do you have a list?"

"That's a question for Shiloh, sir. You should direct it to her."

"Right." He turned reluctantly to her. "Ma'am?"

Her eyes widened in surprise. "Oh…um. The largest dog bed you have, food and water dishes, a very big bag of dogfood—"

"Don't forget toys." Rachel tugged on her sleeve. "Peanut needs toys. And snacks!"

Shiloh nodded. "Add those to the list, please. I had no idea how expensive a dog could be."

"Well, you did adopt the biggest one on the

planet." Rowan chuckled. "You'd better buy a shovel. You'll need one to clean up after her."

"Add a pooper scooper." She sighed and pulled a debit card from her purse.

~

Duke scowled at the sight of the big dog climbing out of the backseat of Shiloh's car. What did she need a dog for? Loud and messy, not to mention he wouldn't be able to sneak into her house and sniff her shampoo, lie on her bed...all the things he'd planned on doing on his next day off.

He cursed and gripped the steering wheel tight enough to make his knuckles ache. He needed to make her understand she belonged to him. Why else would fate bring her back to Misty Hollow? Why else had he never found anyone to take her place? This was all that new deputy's fault. If he hadn't been the one to help Shiloh on her first day into town, maybe Duke would have found her. Then things would've been different. She'd have owed him.

He refused to be cast aside like yesterday's bread. Somehow, he'd convince her to see where her future lay. With him. Duke glanced at the white box on the passenger seat. It had sat there waiting for her to get home from school. Who knew that would be two hours later? Now, he might as well wait until she was in bed, or the dog would sound the alarm.

Cursing again, he drove away, prepared to come back later.

Chapter Seven

Shiloh opened the front door the next morning to find a long white box lying on the porch. Her blood chilled. Instead of picking it up, she returned to the house, locked the door, then called Rowan.

"I'll be there as fast as I can. Stay in the house." He hung up.

"Some watchdog you were last night, Peanut." Shiloh put a hand on the big dog's head. "But, you were snoring pretty loud." And Duke could be very sneaky. All the times he'd snuck to her house late at night to coerce her to come out. She'd hidden behind faded curtains each time, afraid of a repeat of prom night. None of her father's hunting dogs had ever put up a fuss when Duke arrived. He must have a way with dogs.

She groaned and called the school to let them know she'd be in late. Perfect. Late on her third day. What a way to make a good impression.

Her head jerked up at the sound of someone thumping up her porch steps.

"It's me," Rowan called.

Her heart returning to normal, she opened the door and stepped outside. "I didn't touch it."

"That's good." He snapped a pair of gloves over his hands and picked up the box, opening it to reveal a dozen red roses. "No card, but we can guess who left them here. I'll show the sheriff. You okay?"

She nodded. "Annoyed more than anything. Thank you for coming so quickly." She said goodbye to the dog and locked the door. "I need a peephole in my door and security cameras."

"Mention the peephole to Deacon when he comes on Saturday. After school, I'll drop by and show you some good cameras you can order online and run with your Wi-Fi."

"Great. I'll make spaghetti." Rachel's favorite. Shiloh hurried to her car, relieved she'd only miss bus duty and would be in the classroom on time. She parked and rushed into the building. "I'm here." She waved a hand at the ladies in the front office and practically sprinted for her classroom. Five minutes later, she headed outside to collect her students from the playground.

By lunchtime, she already felt as if she'd put in a full day's work. She removed a homemade salad from her lunch box and bought a diet soda from the vending machine. A few minutes later, Susan and Melinda joined her as they had since school started.

"Sorry I was late this morning. Who covered bus duty?" She glanced at each woman.

"I did." Melinda crossed her arms and narrowed her eyes. "You know, Shiloh, some of the parents of your students have been asking Mr. White to transfer their children out of your class."

"Why?" That didn't make sense; she was a good teacher.

"Because of who you are." A sly smile teased at her lips.

"And who would be spreading such stories?" Her neck flushed. "You have no right. I deserve a chance in this town."

Melinda rolled her eyes.

"She's right." Susan shook her head. "Fifteen years ago was a long time. You know she was right about that night. I know you do." She leaned forward and lowered her voice. "Because you've experienced the same thing, haven't you?"

A shadow passed across Melinda's eyes before she turned back to Shiloh. "Mr. White refuses to transfer them, saying you came highly recommended. What have you done to make him think so highly of you after only three days?"

Shiloh leaped to her feet, spilling her soda. The dark liquid spread across the table. "Are you insinuating that I've offered him…to get him on my side?" The heat from her neck spread to her face. "Because you couldn't be more wrong." She grabbed a handful of paper towels from above the sink, then started wiping up the mess. How could anyone be so cruel?

"Don't pay her any attention." Susan glared at Melinda. "She's jealous because she has a thing for the principal, and he likes someone else. And it isn't Shiloh."

"Who is it then?" Melinda's folded arms seemed to tighten.

"Carrie in the office. Now, you can leave Shiloh alone." She gathered up her lunch. "Bring your lunch to my room, Shiloh. The air stinks in here." She flounced from the room.

Shiloh quickly gathered her things and followed, her heart swelling at how Susan had defended her. "Thank you." She sat at one of the students' desks.

"No need to. You've suffered enough at the hands of this town. Needlessly, I might add." She tilted her head. "And it hasn't stopped, has it?"

"Unfortunately, no." Having lost her appetite, she stared at the closed salad container. "It's just going to take time."

"Okay, but stand firm. Don't let anyone run you away again. Not even football-star, arrogant, red-neck Duke. I don't think he'll harm you; he's more of a nuisance. After all, you aren't kids anymore."

Shiloh certainly hoped so, but whenever she saw him, the glimmer of evil in his eyes brought a shudder down her spine. He wouldn't go away quietly.

~

It didn't please Duke one bit to see the deputy's car at Shiloh's again. Since he had his brat with him, they'd be staying for supper. It ought to be Duke sitting at her table.

He watched as Shiloh and the deputy stepped onto the porch. Reynolds pointed from one corner to the other, then at the doorbell. A person didn't have to be a genius to figure out they were discussing security measures.

His fingers curled around the steering wheel as he pretended to have them wrapped around Reynolds's neck. The amount of time those two spent together was bordering on ridiculous. Soon, the residents of Misty Hollow would start thinking of them as a couple. That couldn't happen. No name should be paired with hers except his.

That no-good cousin of his, Melinda, wasn't doing a very good job stirring up trouble in the school. He'd have to come up with a plan B. He drummed his fingers. What, though? The dog was bad enough, but cameras? He'd been lucky last night, sneaking on the porch in his socks so the dog wouldn't hear. There'd be no hiding from cameras.

He pulled the car away from the curb before the neighbor got nosy again. He'd have something figured out when he arrived on Saturday instead of Deacon. For now, there were no cameras.

~

"Those spots and one by the back door should provide plenty of security. You can even snap a photo of the person if you'd like." Rowan ushered Shiloh back inside.

She gave a soft laugh. "I don't really want a photo of Duke."

He knew she was making light of the situation, but cameras would add another level of safety. Anyone approaching the house would be spotted from any direction. He eyed the detached garage. "It might not hurt to have one there, too."

She sighed. "I knew fixing this place up would be expensive, but gee-whiz."

"You can buy the cameras on a monthly payment plan, if that helps."

"It does." Back in the kitchen, she handed him plates and utensils. "Food is ready once the table is set."

Rowan told Rachel to go wash her hands, then set out the dishes. When Rachel's scream rang out from the back of the house, the plate he'd held clattered to the table as he dashed for the bathroom.

His daughter was peering out the back window. "Sasquatch."

"What?" He slid to a stop.

"Out there." She pointed through the slats of the blind. "Bigfoot. I saw him."

"You'd better not be playing games, Rachel." He glanced to where she pointed. "I don't see anything."

"That's because he left. Behind those trees." She washed her hands.

"Why were you looking out the window?"

"Because Peanut left me and huffed at something in the bedroom."

He frowned. "Are you sure?"

"Yep." She dried her hands.

After checking the bedroom where Peanut was not, he headed for the kitchen and told Shiloh what his daughter had said. "I don't think it's anything, but I'm going to make a quick sweep around the yard with the dog. Be back in a few minutes." He never should've let his daughter talk him into that old, based-on-a-true-story, movie about Bigfoot. She'd been obsessed ever since. But, considering the trouble aimed at Shiloh, he had to check things out.

Peanut didn't seem overly interested in anything in the yard. Instead, her nose wrinkled as she turned toward the house, clearly hoping for some spaghetti.

"Come on, girl. Let's check the tree line." He led the dog to where the trees started and stopped to listen. Birds twittered. No snapping of twigs or noise from the dog. Rachel had been imagining things.

Shaking his head, he returned to the house where Shiloh had filled his plate. "Nothing but stories." He shot a sharp look at his daughter. "Just as I suspected."

She shrugged. "I saw him."

"Okay." Shiloh sat down. "You do realize that Bigfoot is very shy, right? He won't like it if you go telling people you saw him. Then, they'll come looking for him. Someone might want to catch him and put him in a cage. Do you want that?"

"No." Her eyes widened. "I won't say anything."

"Genius." Rowan grinned.

Rachel shot a suspicious glance at Shiloh, then dug into her supper, occasionally slipping a noodle to the dog.

When they finished, Rowan helped Shiloh clear off the table, then filled the sink with hot sudsy water. "I'll wash, you dry."

"You really don't have—"

"I know. But, you fed us."

She pulled a dishtowel from a nearby drawer. "You really think it was only Rachel's imagination?"

He arched a brow. "Don't tell me you believe in Bigfoot."

"No, but it could've been a man. Duke, maybe."

"I didn't see anything." He studied her worried face. "You want to come home with me and Rachel? I could sleep on the couch."

"No, I'll be fine with Peanut."

"Can you shoot a gun?"

She nodded. "I don't have one, though. Guess that's another expense I should invest in?"

"I have one you can use in the meantime. I'll bring it by after school tomorrow."

He and Rachel left after finishing the dishes, but instead of heading straight home, he drove to the back side of Shiloh's plot to where an old road, overgrown with weeds now, had once been another way into town. Until the bigger, safer bridge had been built. "Let's take a hike." He opened the door for Rachel. "Just a short one, then home to do homework."

"We're looking for Bigfoot, aren't we?" She slid from the car and dashed into the trees.

"Slow down. I don't want you going in there without me." He rushed to catch up with her, then took her hand.

"What if we find him?" Rachel whispered.

"We'll just watch him. He's shy, remember?" Rowan probably shouldn't be encouraging her, but his mind was on other things. With a sharp eye, he studied the ground around them, noting the disturbance of some dried leaves, the scuff of what looked like a boot, and a full print near a tree. Rowan stood exactly as he thought someone else had. Someone who had had a very clear view of the back of Shiloh's house.

The cameras couldn't arrive too soon for him.

Chapter Eight

Having completed her full first week as a Misty Hollow elementary teacher, Shiloh bounded out of bed Saturday morning. "Come on, Peanut. We have a busy day ahead of us."

Saturday would bring a new roof, if the parts came in. The security cameras would be installed, and the painting crew would start on the outside of the house. As for her, she'd start planting flowers and bushes in the garden. "Very busy weekend for sure," she said to no one but herself. It was all coming together.

With all the renovations, s could almost forget the childhood spent within these four walls. Almost. Not quite. It might have been peaceful at one time, but as far back as Shiloh could remember—from the age of five—her home had been tumultuous. Making it a better place one nail at a time would help her to heal.

She put on a large pot of coffee and carried all but one of her ancient, stained cups left behind in the house and set them on a small table on the porch. There were cookies, but there was also a big dog who'd eat them before the workers arrived. The snacks would have to wait. That taken care of, she fed Peanut and popped a couple slices of bread into the toaster. Shiloh wasn't a big breakfast eater, but she'd need fuel to plant her new foliage. She finished as the first truck rumbled into her yard. Hurrying into the house, she carried the tray of cookies to the porch, set them on the railing, and then went to greet Deacon. "I'm very happy to see you."

"Eager for that roof, are you?" He turned to see a van park next to his truck. "Security people?" Something like worry flitted through his eyes.

"Just an extra precaution for a woman living alone."

"I'm going to put some stronger locks on that house. Install a better door. A small child could kick that one down."

She turned and studied the heavy oak door with clear glass where once there had been a stain where her father had thrown a bottle through it. "Can you get one as close to that one as possible, but stained glass instead of clear?"

"Absolutely. Let me check the back door while we wait for my men to show up."

"Thank you." She headed for the security van. "You have the plans for where I want them?"

"Yes, ma'am. Won't take us but an hour to finish this job."

Shiloh frowned. "If all this hooks up to my Wi-Fi, why are you carrying a large coil of wire?"

"Uh." He pulled a sheet of paper from his pocket. "You'd have to speak to a…Mr. White? These cameras will be wired to your house."

Her principal? She pulled her phone from her purse and stepped away from the others to make her call.

"Everything okay?" His worried voice came through the airwaves.

"Why are you paying for a security system when one was already on order?"

"Well, not just me. I overheard you and Susan talking one day about Duke. I suspect my sister was once a victim of that foul man. Anyway, we pooled together some money. Deputy Reynolds returned your ordered items and put that plus some, I suspect, toward this system."

"Why?" Tears sprang to her eyes. Why would these people want to help her so much?

"Because this man has to be stopped. There aren't many of us not blinded by his charm. We have to stick together."

"Thank you." She didn't know what else to say. People she'd just met or hadn't seen in years believed her and wanted to help prevent anything from happening again.

"Have a good weekend, Shiloh. See you Monday."

She slipped her phone back into her pocket and wiped her eyes with the collar of her tee-shirt. Maybe this place really could be home. She retrieved a shovel from the shed and propped it against the house as she started setting plants where she wanted them. The place needed more trees, bushes, color. She also needed to go to the cellar under the shed and see what needed to be cleaned out down there. It was mostly a tornado shelter, but her father had also used it to store things.

Once the outside of the house was painted, she'd fill the flowerbeds with vibrant colors. While she worked, the painters arrived.

Shiloh returned the coffee pot and cups to the kitchen, informing anyone that wanted a cup or a cookie to help themselves inside the house.

Her yard hummed, workers bustling about like ants. The sound of nails being pounded, a nail gun thumping, and the squeal of a drill combined into a lively melody that made her heart rejoice. There wasn't one part of her house that wasn't being worked on.

Shiloh glanced up the road to see another van parked in front of one of her neighbors' houses. They were neighbors in the sense she could see the house, but too far away for a friendly chat over the backyard fence. Was there someone in the van? No one got in or out of it. No one came out of the house.

She shrugged. It was none of her business. She picked up the shovel and thrust it into the rich clay. A willow oak would grow and shade her bedroom. Over there, a snowball bush would protect the air conditioner. Her mind filled with all the ways she could make the place beautiful.

~

The woman was insane. Duke scowled. He'd made it very clear not only to Shiloh, but also to Deacon. He was supposed to be the only one fixing Shiloh's house. The only one!

Yeah, it would take longer, but that's what he needed. Time. Time for Shiloh to realize the two of them were destined to be together. He thrust the van into drive. It was time to do some convincing. He parked behind a van with the logo of a security company, then shoved his door open. Shoulders up, he marched to where Shiloh was planting a tree.

Her eyes widened, and she stepped back when she saw him. Good. He liked surprising people. "Why aren't you listening to me?"

"What do you mean?" She clutched the shovel.

"How much more clear can I be about being the only one to help you with your house?"

"Think about it. This will finish my home much quicker." She reached for a sapling.

"Let me." He took the tree from her and put it in the hole she'd dug. That should prove to her what a nice guy he could be.

"So, you're not really needed, Duke. Thank you for the offer."

He stiffened. "We'll see about that. If there's no one else to do the work, you'll have to let me." Duke stormed to where Deacon was studying plans on the hood of his truck. "Don't you take a warning, old man?"

"You don't have the authority to make me quit a job you want." The man's face darkened. "Now get out of here."

"Obviously, you don't know who I am. You're too new to this town, but you're about to find out." He curled his fist and drew back.

The short honk of a hand stopped him midair.

He turned and stared through the window at Deputy Reynolds.

~

Rowan shoved his door open and approached the two men. "What's going on here, gentlemen?"

"Larson seems to think he can tell me what job to take or not." Deacon shoved past Duke, knocking into his shoulder.

"Want to start something?" Duke grabbed his arm.

"Get your hands off Deacon." Rowan stepped between them. "Deacon was hired for the job. Sorry if you feel left out, but that's business, right?"

Anger flashed from his eyes. "I'm the one who's supposed to do the job."

"Go on back to your own work. You have a lot on your plate between construction and your mechanic shop. If you get stretched too far, you'll start to lose favor with the town residents because your work will be affected."

Duke didn't look convinced. He looked more like he knew exactly what Rowan was trying to do. "You're right. I have plenty of other things to do than spend my time on this rundown shack. He who comes from the wrong side of the bridge stays on the wrong side of the bridge."

Rowan kept his gaze on him as the man climbed into his van. They locked eyes for a few seconds until Duke backed up and turned around, leaving the property.

"The man's losing it." Deacon shook his head. "He was going to punch me."

"I saw that." He didn't think Duke would have stopped at only one punch. Spotting Shiloh watching from the corner of the house, Rowan headed her way. "Place is busy."

"How did you know you were needed here?" She smiled. "Mind reader?"

"No, just making my rounds and added this road to my route. How long has Duke been here?" He started to lean against the porch railing and stopped right before he got paint on his uniform.

"Five or ten minutes. There's no safe spot outside the house right now. If the kitchen steps weren't concrete, I'd have no way in and out of my house." She grinned, obviously not upset about a minor inconvenience. "Thank you for pitching in toward the security system, but I doubt I'll need something that elaborate."

"Mr. White insisted." He'd told Rowan his suspicions about his sister, but without proof, Rowan couldn't do anything. So, he'd eagerly pitched into the fund to make Shiloh safer. One thing Rowan would do in his spare time was dig into Duke's past. He'd bet Rachel's favorite doll there were a lot of Shilohs and Katy Whites. If he could prove who Duke really was to all those who saw him through glazed glasses, he could stop the man from hurting women. Men like him should not be walking the streets—definitely not working on buildings where women lived.

"He'll come back, you know." Shiloh set a tree near a partially dug hole.

"At least you'll see him coming." He motioned to where the security people were finishing up. "And then there's ferocious Peanut." He laughed at her running in and out of the workers' feet.

Shiloh laughed. "I love her anyway. She's good company."

"I need to get back to work. Remember, I'm only a text away." He flashed her a grin and returned to his car. Rowan parked in the parking lot of Lucy's Diner and punched Duke's name into his computer database. If no one ever said anything about the alleged abuse, he wouldn't find anything. If he struck out here, he'd ask Susan Snodgrass to give him some names. Maybe after all these years, the women would talk.

Why hadn't they talked? What could a teenage Duke have used to keep girls from alerting the authorities? Why had the town rallied behind him after the deal with Shiloh? Did they love their football that much, or did the Larson family have the power to keep people quiet?

The idea left him feeling like a cast member of some gangster movie—the good guy against the whole town. Laughing, he climbed out of his car and strolled toward the diner. He'd fallen in love with Misty Hollow within the first week of living here. The town wasn't bad per se. Just some of the people who resided here were trouble, and he was glad he could have a hand in keeping the town safe.

The bell jingled over the door as he entered. The hostess, a girl still in high school, led him to a small table and handed him a menu.

Rowan didn't need one. He always had whatever the day's special was.

"That was uncool, man." Duke exited the small hall that led to the restrooms and stopped at Rowan's table.

"What was?" He adopted his impassive-cop face.

"Disrespecting me in front of those workers." He crossed his arms, the sleeves of his shirt straining under the man's biceps.

"You didn't belong there. Shiloh Sloan chose somebody else."

Duke rolled his head on his shoulders, then planted his palms flat on the table. "Shiloh isn't up for bids. That wouldn't be very good for the other…bidder."

"Are you threatening me, Larson?" Rowan straightened to level narrowed eyes at the brute.

"Promising is more like it." He grinned and clapped Rowan on the shoulder. "The future looks promising indeed."

Maybe so, but not for Duke. Rowan was going to make sure the man was knocked off his high horse. Rowan did not intimidate. Duke would realize that soon enough.

Chapter Nine

Shiloh handed Deacon a check that used half of her savings and stepped back to survey the outside of her house. "Sure looks good."

A coat of new white paint had done wonders, along with a bright blue front door and shutters and a shiny white metal roof.

She turned to the older man with a smile. "Ready to redo my kitchen and bathroom?"

He chuckled. "You send me a picture of how you want them to look, and I'll pick up the supplies. Enjoy your weekend, Miss Sloan. The yard's looking nice, too."

Shiloh was proud of her hard work. "Want to help me bring the rocking chairs out of the shed, Peanut?" She'd bought them a few days ago but wanted to wait until the house was finished before setting up her porch.

A man yelled for her attention.

She turned, Peanut stepping in front of her. "Can I help you?"

"I'm Nick Nelson, a neighbor. There's this man…drives a white van. He sits in front of my house for a while every day staring down this way. I thought maybe he was on his break from all the work going on down here." His brow furrowed. "Looks good, by the way. Anyway, I don't think he's one of the workers."

"He's not." Her voice turned hoarse.

"Is he bothering you? I can call the cops next time he shows up."

"That's not necessary. I don't want to get you involved." She didn't trust Duke not to hurt someone just to make a point to her. "He's nothing more than a nuisance."

"Are you sure? Because as a woman living alone, you can't be too careful. My wife and I don't like him sitting out there."

"He'll get bored with it soon enough." No, he wouldn't. Duke would remain a hovering threat until someone stopped him. That was something that would never happen. This town didn't mess with the Larson family. Never had. "Thank you for your concern." She pasted on a smile, then headed for the shed.

By the time she'd finished making the porch feel welcoming, the sun sat high in the sky. Her stomach growled, reminding her it had been a while since breakfast. "How about we have lunch at the diner? I heard they've set tables outside since the weather turned nice so people can eat out there. I bet they won't mind you being outside."

Peanut's tail thumped the ground.

Shiloh locked up the house and set the alarm. Rowan had been correct in saying she'd sleep better with the security system turned on. With the cameras and Peanut, it wouldn't be easy for anyone to sneak into her home. She drove across the bridge and into town, parking in a spot near the picnic tables. While waiting for someone to bring her a menu, she looped Peanut's leash around the table leg.

"Hey!" Rachel darted across the lot. "We can eat together."

Shiloh smiled at the embarrassed look on her father's face. "That's fine by me."

"Sorry. Sometimes, my daughter doesn't know her boundaries." He ruffled the girl's hair. "I like to bring her out to eat on my days off." He scratched Peanut's ear. "How's the house?"

"The outside is complete. Please, sit." She thought about telling him what her neighbor had said that morning but decided against it. All Duke did, creepy as it was, was watch her from the top of the hill. She hadn't spoken to him in a week. Maybe he'd already realized she meant it when she said she wanted nothing to do with him.

The arrival of their server broke off her thoughts, reminding her she wasn't alone. She was having lunch with friends. Living alone tended to make her stay to herself too much. Maybe she needed to get out more and not just go to work.

"The special, please." Rowan didn't glance at his menu.

"What is the special?" Shiloh glanced up. "Do you ever order anything from the menu?"

"Today's special is a BLT with Texas fries." He grinned. "And no, I usually order whatever the special is. That way, I don't lock myself into ordering the same thing all the time."

"What if you don't like it?"

"I've always liked it so far."

She laughed. "Okay. I'll have the special, too."

"Popcorn chicken for me," Rachel piped up.

"A plain burger for my dog, please." Shiloh returned her menu.

The server nodded and returned to the building.

"I like the tables outside." Shiloh put a hand on her dog's head. "This gives me somewhere to take her."

"The two of you would love the hiking path around Misty Lake." Rowan put an arm around his daughter's shoulders. "The park offers several paths to take, depending on your time limit. Anywhere from one mile to five."

"I'll do that." Tomorrow. A walk around the lake would be the perfect thing for a Sunday afternoon.

Her smile faded as Duke pulled into the parking lot. Spotting them, he parked next to Shiloh's car and stared at them through the windshield.

"Ignore him." Rowan's eyes hardened.

Peanut growled deep in her throat.

Shiloh's heart leaped into her throat when Duke got out of his van and approached the table.

~

"Deputy." Duke's lip curled in a sneer. "Shiloh. Nice day for a picnic."

"What do you want?" Rowan tried to keep the growl from his voice. No need to frighten Rachel.

"Just stopping to grab something to eat." He eyed the empty spot next to Shiloh.

"That spot is for the dog." Rowan grinned. "There's an empty table over there."

Duke's eyes narrowed. "I prefer to eat inside." He continued into the building and sat at a table near the front window.

"Great." Shiloh crossed her arms. "He can still watch us."

"Not if we change tables." He took Rachel's hand and led her to a different table.

"Did something happen between the two of you?" Shiloh sat across from him, her gaze landing on where Rachel played with Peanut in a patch of grass.

"Me and Duke? Nothing more than usual. He warned me to stay away from you." Rowan laughed. "That sort of behavior doesn't go over well with me." He folded his hands on the top of the table. "What's up with him and this town?"

She shrugged. "I grew up here knowing no one bothered the Larsons, but I never knew why. Maybe they're one of the founding families and deserve respect?"

"It has to be more than that." He glanced at the building. "I'll talk to the sheriff. Since I've been working and living here, I didn't know anything about Duke until you showed up." Which meant her arrival had reawakened the monster inside, or the man had simply been sneakier about his dirty deeds.

"I wasn't going to say anything, but—" She stopped as their server approached. The girl did a fancy bit of footwork in order not to get tangled up with a very excited Peanut.

"I'm so sorry." Shiloh grabbed the dog's collar. "Bad girl. Sit."

"It's okay. I like dogs." She set their food on their table and left.

"You were saying?" Rowan arched a brow.

"It'll wait." She bobbed her head toward Rachel.

He nodded, knowing whatever she wanted to say had something to do with Larson. He hadn't dug anything up during his internet searches, but he'd keep at it until something unearthed. It might not hurt to have another talk with June and a few of the other old-timers. He'd have to be careful, though, that no one tipped off Larson.

Rachel gobbled down her popcorn chicken and returned to the grass with the dog.

"My neighbor came to me this morning and informed me that Duke sits in a van at the top of the hill in front of this man's home and watches my house." She gathered up their garbage. "I'm not terribly worried because of my new security and Peanut, but his presence bothers my neighbor."

"I'll stop by there Monday and talk to him. See if he wants to file a complaint."

"Too many people involved will make Duke angry." A worried look crossed her face. "He might do more than just watch."

"The more people who don't bow down to him, the fewer people there are who will back him up." He called to Rachel that it was time to go home. "We'll keep a sharp eye on him."

Duke climbed into his van and tossed them a salute before backing from the spot and driving away. Yes, they'd be watching him very closely.

When Rowan went to turn onto the street where he lived with Rachel, Duke's vehicle blocked the way. The man stood next to his van, feet planted, arms crossed.

Rowan threw his truck into park. "Stay here, Rachel." He shoved his door open and went to stand about six feet from the man. "You're blocking the road."

"What do ya know?" He pretended to look around. "I sure am."

"What do you want?"

"I thought maybe you didn't understand me when I told you to stay away from my woman."

"She isn't your woman. Shiloh can be friends with anyone she wants."

"Friends?" He tilted his head. "Is that what you are? Well, I don't believe in men and women being just friends." He pushed away from his van. "I'll tell you one more time, Deputy. Stay away."

"Do you realize I can arrest you for threatening me?" Rowan clenched his jaw.

"People around here don't go against me. You'd do well to remember that." He glanced to where Rachel hung out the window of the truck. "Yep. Best to remember." He climbed into his truck. "Mind moving? You're blocking my way."

Rowan moved out of the man's way, then drove the rest of the way home. At the first opportunity, he'd arrest the man, but he needed to make sure the charges would stick. And when he did arrest the man, he wanted to make sure Duke Larson was locked up for a very long time.

"I don't like that man, Daddy." Rachel slid from the truck.

"Neither do I, sweetie, and I want you to stay away from him, okay? Let me know if you see him anywhere near you."

"Okay." She skipped up the porch steps.

Before following, Rowan gave a good hard look down his drive. Not seeing any sign of Larson, he entered the house and locked the door before stepping into his office and calling the sheriff.

"He's threatened you twice, and he's still a free

man?" The sheriff chuckled. "I guess that means you have something up your sleeve."

"I do." He told him of his suspicions regarding alleged sexual assaults on several women in Misty Hollow over the years. "I want to find out why these people are so afraid of him, how many victims there are, then I intend to collect enough evidence to rid the town of him. Right now, that means he needs to think he can't be touched."

"The fact he's threatened law enforcement is enough reason to bring him in, but if you want to keep digging, keep a file, and the department will work with you. I'll give a briefing on Monday to watch Larson without tipping him off."

"I appreciate that, sir."

"Word of warning, though." The sheriff paused. "You have a little girl that man can use as a bargaining chip. Be careful."

Chapter Ten

Shiloh stowed a cooler and an old quilt in the trunk of her car. "Come on, Peanut. Let's have a picnic."

The dog tore her gaze from the hill up the road and bounded into the backseat.

As Shiloh drove away from the house, she glanced in the rearview mirror and marveled at the transformation new paint and some boards could do. The house no longer resembled the shack she'd seen on the first day back. Instead, a cozy cottage waited to provide respite at the end of a long day of work. She smiled and waved at the neighbor who had mentioned Duke watching her and headed for the lake. Nothing would mar the beauty of this day—she wouldn't allow it.

Spotting Duke in the parking lot of the mechanic shop, she drove by without glancing his way. Maybe if she pretended he didn't exist, he'd realize she meant what she said. There could be nothing between them. He'd ruined that years ago.

She did wave at Rowan sitting in his patrol car. The man had proven to be a great friend. If not for him, she'd still be painting. Friend? She frowned. What if she encouraged him to be more than friends? Did Rowan want a relationship after the death of his wife? Why hadn't such a handsome man, a wonderful father, remarried? Shiloh shrugged. It was none of her business, although if he did enter the dating world, she wanted on his list. She chuckled. "Hear that, Peanut? Now that I'm settled back into Misty Hollow, I'm dreaming of romance. Pathetic, aren't I?"

The dog licked the back of her neck, turning the chuckle into a giggle.

"You have been my best investment in years, girl." She couldn't imagine life without the silly canine.

The car's tires crunched as she pulled into the gravel parking lot of Misty Lake Park. She opened the back door to let Peanut out, then retrieved the items from the trunk. "Let's find the perfect spot to watch the water—hopefully, away from people." After a week of teaching and days of workmen swarming around her place, she could use a few hours of solitude.

She led the way down a well-worn dirt path until she found a patch of grass near the lake's shore. The afternoon sun kissed the water with diamonds. A few fishing boats floated in the middle of the lake. Geese swam and fished. She hadn't seen anything more idyllic in a long time.

After spreading the quilt, she sat and opened the cooler. She poured some water into a bowl for Peanut, then poured herself a drink before leaning back on her elbows to simply be. Closing her eyes, she lifted her face to the sun.

A rustle behind her alerted her to the fact her dog had left the blanket. "Don't go far. I don't want to lose you." Shiloh lay on her side, using her arm as a pillow and watched Peanut nose around in the bushes.

She woke to deep barking. Eyes popping open, she sat up and stared into the trees. "Peanut, come." Silly dog. Shiloh stood and followed the barking.

Hackles raised, Peanut barked in the direction of the parking lot.

A trail of red rose petals left a trail in that direction.

Shiloh's heart leaped into her throat.

Maybe the petals were left as a marriage proposal. She glanced around hoping to see a young woman following the trail.

"Are they still here, girl? The person who left the flowers?" She swallowed against a dry throat. Her heart thumped so hard she could see her chest move with the beat.

A cloud passed across the sun. She shuddered, the peace of the day gone.

~

Stupid dog. Duke had wanted to get closer, intending to watch Shiloh sleep. She'd looked so beautiful, so vulnerable, lying there, the sun highlighting her hair.

He'd wanted to leave the roses at her side, and he almost had, until the dog stepped from the trees and started barking. He'd had no choice but to retreat and leave his message in the form of scattered petals.

In order to convince Shiloh she belonged to him, he needed to court her properly, woo her with romantic things. The dog would pose a problem, though. Duke drummed his fingers on the steering wheel. He liked animals and didn't want to harm her dog. Somehow, he needed to make friends with the beast. Let the dog see he meant no harm so he could get close to Shiloh.

Treats? The occasional steak bone? He'd think of something.

Catching sight of Shiloh returning with the quilt and cooler, he left the parking area and found a side road to sit and wait for her to pass. He'd be her shadow as much as time permitted. It had made his heart glad to see her at the lake alone and not with Deputy Reynolds. Maybe there wasn't anything between the two of them after all.

If they did get close, he'd find a way to end the relationship. If he couldn't have Shiloh, then no one could. She'd belonged to him ever since that night fifteen years ago when he'd claimed her. Nothing would change that.

Oh, she'd cried and struggled, but only because she didn't realize what they had. Now that she was grown, a mature adult, things would be very different. She'd see. When the time was right, he'd show her how much they belonged together. One night together, and she wouldn't want anyone else.

~

Rowan frowned to see Shiloh returning from the lake so soon. He'd expected her to be out there for several hours. A glance at his watch showed a little over an hour. He almost followed her home but decided against it. She knew to call him if she needed him. On his agenda for the day was a visit to June Mayfield. If anyone knew what the Larsons held over the town, she would. Pulling away from the curb, he drove the couple of blocks to the old woman's house and parked out front.

She waved from the rocking chair she sat on.

"Come on in. I've tea and cookies."

He grinned and headed up the steps. "I have a feeling you always do just in case."

"Absolutely. Help me out of this chair." She held out a hand.

He took her fragile one in his and helped her to her feet. "Can I ask you some questions?"

"You sure can, although I might not answer if they're too personal." She entered the house ahead of him.

"The questions aren't about you, ma'am."

"Then I'll answer. Have a seat on the sofa. I'll be right in." She bustled into the kitchen. A few minutes later, she entered with a silver tray.

Rowan took the tray from her and set it on the coffee table. "I'll pour."

"Thank you." She settled onto a chair across from him. "Who do you want to know about?"

"Duke Larson."

Her brow lowered. "You've already asked me about him and Shiloh."

"This is more about his family." He poured the tea and handed her a cup, then offered the plate of cookies. "Why is the Larson family immune to the consequences of their actions?"

She tilted her head. "Do you know the old saying, 'snitches get stitches'?"

"Yes." He took a cookie and settled against the back of the sofa.

"Well, it used to be that way when Duke's grandfather ran this town. Then, Duke's father let things slide a bit. That caused a rift between him and his father. Then, Duke came along with the same personality type as the senior Larson. The old man took Duke under his wing. Heaven help anyone who came against that boy."

"This is the twenty-first century. Why haven't people taken a stand? Why hasn't the sheriff?"

"Things have been pretty calm since Shiloh left. That was before Sheriff Westbrook's time." She sipped her tea. "Maybe you're the very man to change things around here."

He pressed his lips together and shook his head. "Call me a coward, but if Duke is as bad as you say, I can't risk Rachel."

"I don't think he'd harm a child, and you're anything but a coward, Deputy. Worrying over your child proves you're a good father."

He tried to be. With a sigh, he finished the cookie. "I don't understand the mindset of the people of this town. Shiloh can't be the only woman Larson has assaulted. I need to find the others and see whether they'd come forward about the abuse."

"Maybe Shiloh knows. She's the only one who was brave enough to say anything." Furrows creased her features. "I fear things will get worse for dear Shiloh."

So did Rowan. "I'll do my best to protect her. The sheriff has asked that I keep an eye on her as much as I can, but Larson isn't going to back down without a fight."

"Then you'd best be ready for that fight because you're correct. Duke Larson won't quit. With his father and grandfather both in hell where they belong, he's alone. He'll be a cornered animal." Her expression turned grave.

Rowan's eyes widened at her words. "I'll find a way to make him see reason."

"Let me say one more thing about Duke Larson. He can't help who he is. That man has been groomed to believe he's king his entire life. He's been taught to take what he wants and hang the consequences. His daddy and grandfather, too. He doesn't know any other way to behave. But you stay optimistic, Deputy Reynolds. It's cute." She grinned, then sobered again. "Be careful. Watch your girls very closely."

He liked thinking of Shiloh as his girl. He pushed to his feet. Maybe he'd ask her on a real date sometime. For now, he'd invite her to join him and Rachel at the diner for supper. Feel her out on any other women Larson might have assaulted. "Thank you, June."

"Not sure I was much help. I think you already suspected the town's afraid of Duke. One would think with new people arriving, some of that power would've left him."

"I guess those people haven't run across him yet."

"*Against* him, you mean."

When she started to get up, he motioned for her to stay. "I can see myself out. Thank you for the tea and cookies."

"Come see me anytime. Bring your little girl."

With a nod and a promise to return, Rowan returned to his car. He sent Shiloh a text inviting her to join him and Rachel for supper. When she responded with a yes, he continued his patrols for the day. As he worked, his mind whirled at how one family could control an entire town with the threat of violence. Most of the residents didn't know the Larson family, or Duke, as anything more than a mechanic and construction worker. But those who did, would not cross him.

That fact would make bringing him to justice all that much harder. Not one to back down from a challenge, Rowan would find a way to stop Duke while keeping Rachel and Shiloh safe.

The man couldn't be allowed to hurt any more women.

Chapter Eleven

The petals on the path by the lake still rattled Shiloh as she pulled into the diner's parking lot. Thankfully, Rowan and Rachel had chosen an outside table so Peanut wouldn't have to stay in the car.

Shiloh pasted on a smile, wishing she'd stayed at home, and exited the vehicle. Being law enforcement, Rowan was sure to see something had her bothered.

He frowned as she sat across from him. "How was your afternoon at the lake?"

"Great." She reached for the menu from the server. "Beautiful day."

"You weren't there long."

She narrowed her eyes. "How would you know that?"

"I saw you coming and going." He grinned. "This town isn't that big. My patrol is more like driving in circles. I was on Main Street when you left and again when you returned."

"Hmm." She pretended to study the menu. The last thing she wanted was to bring up the subject of the rose petals. They might not have anything to do with her. She most likely overreacted. Not unthinkable considering Duke.

"I'll take the special." Rowan returned the menu to the server. "I'm a sucker for pork chops."

"That sounds good. I'll take the same." Shiloh handed the menu back unread. "Add a burger patty for my dog, please."

"Can I play with Peanut?" Rachel slid from her seat.

"Of course." Shiloh smiled her way. "She loves playing with you."

Once his daughter was out of earshot, Rowan's grin faded. "What happened today?"

"I'm sure it's nothing. Really." She picked at a stain on the wooden table, scraping it with her fingernail.

He put his hand over hers. "You don't have to tell me, but I'm here if you need someone to talk to. You know that, right?"

She nodded and sighed. "I fell asleep by the lake and woke to Peanut barking. When I went to investigate, I found the path strewn with rose petals that led to the parking lot. I'm sure it was just a marriage proposal."

He straightened. "You didn't see any sign of Larson or his van?"

"No. Besides, why would he hide?" The man didn't have a problem approaching her.

His gaze remained locked on hers for several seconds before answering. "I spoke with June Mayfield regarding Duke and his family."

"What? Why?" Goosebumps broke out on her arms. "You could ignite a fire, Rowan."

"So I've heard." He crossed his arms. "Are there other women, Shiloh?"

She hitched her chin, eyes flashing. "I believe so, yes."

"Would they come forward?"

"I doubt it. They haven't yet."

"Will you give me their names?"

She shook her head. "They wish to remain in the background. Why do you care about something that happened so long ago?"

"Because crimes were committed, and no justice was served. As law enforcement, it's my job—"

"Don't worry about the past. It's over and done with. Let's work on convincing Duke I don't want to be his girlfriend." That word sounded so high schoolish coming from her lips.

Rowan didn't look convinced. "I'm not going to stop trying to find a way to put Larson behind bars for what he did to you."

Tears stung her eyes. "It was a long time ago. I've moved past all that pain." *Liar.* The pain and fear burned as raw today as fifteen years ago.

"I care about you, Shiloh. No one should've had to go through what you went through."

"I agree, but I did, and I'm stronger for it." She sat back to allow room for the server to set her food in front of her. "Peanut." She tossed the dog a burger as Rachel climbed onto the bench next to her father. Her heart warmed to know Rowan cared for her, but Shiloh couldn't let digging up a very unpleasant past disrupt the new life she'd made for herself. Best to concentrate on keeping Duke at arm's length until reality sunk in.

While they ate, she regaled Rowan with tales of her students, taking comfort from the warmth of his laughter at some of the kids' shenanigans. "Hopefully, they won't grow up to take rides in your car."

"I take rides in Daddy's car." Rachel frowned. "It's fun. Sometimes, I turn on the lights."

"Shh. That's a secret." He winked at Shiloh. "I don't think the sheriff would approve, but it doesn't make sense to go home and switch vehicles just to pick her up from school, then switch back when I return to work."

"It probably doesn't matter in a small town like Misty Hollow." After all, folks weren't as uptight as in some places. When she was finished eating, she tossed her napkin on her plate. "I'd best head home. I have papers to grade."

"Thank you for joining us."

"It's better than eating alone." She smiled and got to her feet. Shiloh slowed as she passed the neighbor's house at the top of the hill. Something didn't look right. She stopped and stared at the front door left open a few inches. It didn't mean anything, right? The couple had most likely stepped out to do some yard work.

She waited a few more minutes. When she still didn't see them, she pushed open her door. "Stay, Peanut." The dog had jumped out the window before Shiloh reached the front porch and positioned herself between Shiloh and the front door. "Move, silly." The hair on Shiloh's arms stood at attention. Something was definitely wrong. "Hello?" She pushed the door open further. "It's your neighbor, Shiloh Sloan."

Peanut whined and leaned against her leg.

Taking a deep breath, Shiloh moved down the short hall and stopped at a bedroom door. She knocked, then pushed it open. A scream spewed from her mouth as she dashed from the house, pulling her phone from her pocket. In the safety of her car, she dialed Rowan.

~

"Hey, Shiloh." Rowan sent Rachel to the living room and stepped outside to take the call. "Is everything okay?" She was rambling with a mixture of gasps and sobs. "Slow down, sweetheart. I can't understand you."

"Neighbors. The Nelsons. Dead." She gulped. "At the top of the hill."

"I'll be there as soon as my babysitter arrives." He hung up and called Alice who promised to be there in five minutes. While he waited, he unlocked his gun safe and removed his weapon and badge. "Rachel, sweetie, I have to go to work. Alice is coming. You be good for her, okay?"

Without looking away from the show on the television, his daughter nodded. His leaving at the drop of a hat wasn't new to her.

Alice arrived right on time allowing him to head over immediately. Shiloh sat in her car at the top of the hill, her head resting against the steering wheel. She glanced up with tear-filled eyes. "It's horrible. You'll find them in the master bedroom at the back of the house."

"Stay here. I'll be right back." He removed his weapon and entered the house, his heart rate increasing.

In the master bedroom, the couple had been tied to the headboard, their heads bound so they couldn't move. Their noses had been cut off and placed on their chests.

Rowan almost jumped out of his skin when the man's eyes opened. He was alive! "Hold on, sir. I'm calling for help." He stepped into the hall and called for an ambulance before returning and cutting the man and his wife free.

The woman squirmed and screamed as he freed her.

"Please, ma'am, remain still. An ambulance is coming."

"He said he was cutting off our noses to show us what being a nosy neighbor meant." Mr. Nelson gagged. "Can we put our noses on ice or something?"

"How long ago did this happen?"

He shrugged. "I don't know."

"I'll get some ice." He didn't think it would do any good, but if it gave the Nelsons hope, it was the least he could do. On his way to the kitchen, he called the sheriff who said he'd be there in less than ten minutes.

Rowan found a baggie and filled it with ice. He wasn't a squeamish man, but the thought of picking up the severed noses made his stomach churn. He cast a look out the front door to make sure Shiloh still sat in her car, tossed her a wave, then returned to the bedroom where Mr. Nelson put the noses in the baggie. Rowan set the baggie at the foot of the bed.

"Can you describe your attacker, sir?"

"He wore a mask." Mr. Nelson put an arm around his wife's shoulder. Blood continued to pour down their chins and onto their chests. "I'm starting to get cold, Deputy."

"It's shock." He grabbed a crocheted blanket from the back of a chair and draped it over their shoulders. Where was the ambulance? These two were going to bleed to death.

There. Sirens split the air. A couple of minutes later, two paramedics rushed into the house. "In the back." Rowan stepped into the hall to let them do their job as the sheriff strode toward him.

He filled him in.

"The perp cut off their noses?"

"Yes, sir. They couldn't give me a description, but my money is on Larson."

The sheriff's eyes narrowed. "Why's that?"

"Because Mr. Nelson reported Larson's van sitting outside his house on multiple occasions while the man watched Shiloh's place. The victim also said the noses were cut off because they were nosy neighbors. Who else would think that of them?"

"It's a good assumption, but we can't do anything without proof. Get me that proof."

"Yes, sir." There wasn't anything he'd like more than to have current, solid evidence against Larson.

"Send Miss Sloan home. She doesn't need to be here when the Nelsons are wheeled out. The woman's seen enough." Sheriff Westbrook stepped into the bedroom.

Rowan moved to Shiloh's car. "You can go now. I'll follow you home."

"It's right there."

"Humor me." He wanted to make sure her house was clear before she entered. Yes, she had cameras, but a snip of the electrical wires would make them useless.

"It was Duke, wasn't it?" Wide eyes looked back at him from a pale face.

"We don't know that for sure."

"But, you think it is, don't you?"

"My gut says so, yes. Since the Nelsons are still alive, I'm hoping to find out for sure." He patted the car. "Go on, now. I'll be right behind you."

She nodded and pulled away from the curb.

At the house, he made her stay on the porch while he entered first. Some of the tension left his shoulders when he disarmed the alarm. Realizing it wasn't likely an intruder hid anywhere, he still searched all the rooms and closets before letting the dog in. When Peanut didn't seem disturbed, he waved Shiloh inside.

"Thank you." She set her purse and keys on the kitchen table. "I don't think I'll get that sight out of my mind for a long time. So much blood."

He didn't tell her the reason for the blood. "Do you want me to stay for a while?"

"No, I'll do some work, have a glass of wine, and go to sleep once I settle down." Her gaze lifted. "I'm safe here." She smiled. "In the past, heading across that bridge didn't seem like it led to safety, but now it's my sanctuary. You had a big part in that, Rowan. I'm grateful."

He prayed her trust wasn't misplaced. He'd done all he could to make her safe in her home. Now, it was up to him to make her safe in Misty Hollow.

Chapter Twelve

Shiloh woke Monday morning with eyes gritty from lack of sleep. She couldn't get the vision of the Nelsons out of her mind. To think they'd survived was beyond her.

She grabbed her bag and set the alarm. "Watch the house, girl. I'll be home right after school." Maybe she could apply to have Peanut licensed as a therapy dog and take her to school with her. The students would love her.

At lunch, she sat at a table with Susan and Melinda as she did almost every school day. She jerked upright at Melinda's words. "Can you repeat that?"

The other teacher frowned as if Shiloh was dense. "The Nelsons. Someone cut off their noses, but I have it on good authority they were sewn back on."

Their noses were cut off? Shiloh shuddered. She'd assumed they'd been beaten bloody. What had been done to them was beyond barbaric.

"I also heard that you were the one who found them?" Melinda tilted her head. "You're always right in the thick of things, aren't you?"

"Are you insinuating I had something to do with their attack?" Her brows must be in her hairline.

"No, just stating…" Her words tailed off when Duke entered the room.

All three women lowered their heads, concentrating on their lunches. Maybe if they didn't acknowledge him, he'd go away.

"Three gorgeous ladies. How did I get so lucky?"

Shiloh kept her head down. Was that a spot of blood on his shoe? The work boots definitely had a rust drop on them. She yanked her gaze to his. "Where were you yesterday afternoon?"

Surprise shone in his eyes. "Working, why? You thinking about me?" One corner of his mouth curled. "I like that."

Not in the way he thought. Shiloh shook her head. "Don't flatter yourself. What's that on your shoe?"

"What? That spot? Barn paint." He laughed. "Did you think it was blood? You're a funny woman, Shiloh. See you ladies around. I'm here helping the maintenance worker all day." He gave a salute and strolled from the room.

"Are you crazy?" Susan hissed. "Are you trying to antagonize him?"

"No, but someone attacked the Nelsons. My guess is Duke." She'd tell Rowan the next time they spoke.

"He doesn't respect women," Melinda said, "but he's not a murderer."

"They didn't die." Appetite gone, Shiloh put the uneaten portion of her sandwich back in her lunch bag. "Duke is known to attack those who oppose him. Mr. Nelson called the authorities on Duke last week." She pushed to her feet. "I'm going to watch him very closely."

"Closer than he watches you?" Melinda arched a

brow. "You're playing with fire."

"Well, at least you're no longer accusing me of wanting him." She headed for her classroom but froze in the doorway.

Duke stood on a ladder replacing a bulb. "Come on in. You won't be in my way."

No way would she be in a room alone with him. She'd put her lunch away and head to the playground.

"Cute room. I wish I had had a pretty teacher like you when I was kid. I might not have ditched so much."

Without responding, she opened her bottom desk drawer and dropped her lunch bag inside. Squaring her shoulders, she headed for the door.

"It's getting old—you playing hard to get, Shiloh." He climbed down the ladder. "The sooner you realize your fate, the better for everyone."

She shot him a look, her legs growing weak at the harshness on his face. She hurried toward the door only to be stopped when Duke grabbed her arm. "Get your hands off of me." She yanked free. "Touch me again, and I'll call the sheriff." She reached the door when his voice sounded.

"Wake up, Shiloh, before something happens to wake you up,"

With his threat hovering over her, she walked on trembling legs to the playground. She leaned against the brick wall of the school and watched her students play a game of kickball.

What she needed to find was evidence that Duke attacked the Nelsons. That very evidence could be the spot on his boot. He wouldn't be able to harass her or harm anyone else if he sat behind bars. Rather than wait until she saw Rowan, she sent him a text about the spot on the boot.

But how? She couldn't—wouldn't—pretend she'd "woken up." Duke would demand a physical relationship—something she would never agree to. He'd already taken away her innocence. No longer the naïve, rebellious teen, she was now a grown woman with the ability to bring him down.

She could break into his house. Take a day off work and sneak in while he worked. If caught, though, the consequence would be severe. Unless she got caught by the authorities. Then they'd give her a slap on the hand, a warning. Since the department knew of the danger Duke posed to her, they might be lenient on her punishment. Would it be worth it? Yeah, maybe.

She focused her attention on her students. Would she lose her job if caught? Most definitely if she got arrested. Her shoulders slumped. She had a lot of serious thinking to do.

The bell rang signaling the end of lunch recess. She stood waiting for her students to line up. When they reached her room, relief flooded through her to see Duke had done his work and moved on.

A boy in her class raised his hand.

"Yes, Ryan?"

"Are you dating my cousin, Duke? He said you were."

"No, I am not." She opened the door to the school. Duke was spreading rumors now? People would believe him. She'd been down this road before. Only this time, she wouldn't run.

~

Duke would resort to scare tactics if that's what it took to force Shiloh to open her eyes. He shouldered open another classroom and set up the ladder.

Twice a year he helped the maintenance worker with bulbs and air filters. If he worked slowly, he could stretch the job to two days—two days he'd get to see Shiloh in the afternoons. He needed the mornings for work at the garage.

Duke had enjoyed their little sparring session in the cafeteria. Seeing she still had spunk made the chase that much more enjoyable.

She also wasn't stupid. Because he'd been negligent about cleaning his boots properly, she'd spotted Nelson's blood. What would she do with her suspicion? Go to the sheriff or keep it to herself?

The Nelsons wouldn't know it was him. He'd disguised his voice and covered his face. He doubted they'd have looked at his boots. No, they'd been terrified and followed his orders, even when he told them to lie on the bed so he could tie them up.

Oh, the look in their eyes when he'd pulled his knife. The shriek that had erupted from the woman when he made the cut. The cries of her husband. He was the one responsible. He and his nosiness.

While he didn't think they knew the identity of their attacker, he needed to make sure they didn't say anything if they did. A threatening letter would work. He'd let them know that talking would result in more than the loss of a nose. They'd find themselves buried.

~

Interesting and could be very important. After reading the text from Shiloh, Rowan knocked on the door to the hospital room where the Nelsons were recovering from their attack.

"Come in." They both sat upright in their beds. Mr.

Nelson pressed the remote and turned off the television. "We made the news. Not exactly how I'd pictured it if it ever happened." His voice sounded stuffy from the bandage covering the center of his face.

"Mind if I ask you a few questions? I didn't feel as if you could yesterday." Rowan sat in a guest chair.

"Sure, but I can't tell you anything but what I said yesterday. The man wore a ski mask." He glanced at his wife. "Can you add anything?"

She shook her head. "I was too frightened to notice much of anything." Tears welled in her eyes. "I thought we were going to die."

"Did you see any of his skin?" Rowan pulled a notepad from his jacket pocket.

"Caucasian," Mr. Nelson said. "Dark hair on his arms. I could tell when he cut me. His voice sounded weird. As if he disguised it."

"What can you tell me about his size and build? The color of his eyes?"

"Dark eyes," the woman said. "Shark eyes?" She closed her and turned her head. "I'll never forget them."

"Large build." Mr. Nelson nodded. "Seemed familiar, but then again, I wasn't exactly thinking straight. Broad shoulders."

"Do you think you'd recognize him if you saw him?"

He shrugged. "Maybe."

"Would you be able to come in this afternoon and try picking him out of a lineup?" He'd heard they were being released and could pick Duke up because of the physical description.

"We can try."

"I'll send a car for you. After the lineup, the deputy

will take you home." He stood. "Thank you."

After receiving the sheriff's go-ahead, he drove to the garage to bring Larson in. He wasn't at the garage. Rowan drove around until he spotted the man's van at the school. He glanced at the clock on his dashboard. School would be out in thirty minutes. Larson would probably leave before that. Rowan settled in to wait and sent Shiloh a text asking if she'd take Rachel home with her.

She replied with a yes seconds before Larson exited the building. As the man pulled from the parking lot, Rowan followed, staying back a ways. He didn't want to nab him at the school or any other public place. If Rowan was wrong about the man, although he didn't think he was, he didn't want to embarrass him.

Larson pulled into the lot of his garage. He turned and scowled as Rowan drove up alongside him. "Afternoon, Deputy."

"Duke." Rowan slid out. "I need to take you in for a lineup."

"For what?' The man's face darkened.

"You match the physical description of the man who attacked the Nelsons. We're bringing in four others." He grinned. "If you're innocent, you have nothing to worry about."

"You saying I hurt those people?"

"I'm not saying anything like that." He opened the back door to his car. "Please."

"I'll follow you. I'm not getting in your car."

"If you don't follow me, I'll arrest you for obstruction of justice."

"I said I would, didn't I?" Larson climbed into his van.

Rowan shrugged and slammed the door. The man knew the consequences if he didn't follow.

At the office, he followed Larson inside and put him in the interrogation room until the other four men were brought in. He watched with amusement through the two-way mirror as Duke paced, every line of his body rigid. He'd give a hundred dollars to know what was going through his head.

The other two deputies, Deputy Shea Hatchett and Deputy Joey Hudson joined him. "He doesn't look happy," Matchett pointed out.

"No. I'm sure he'll try and get back at me some way."

Hudson clapped him on the shoulder. "We got your back."

"Thanks." He entered the room and retrieved Duke, then led him to where the lineup would take place.

The other four men looked as unhappy as Larson did. "This won't take long, folks." He moved to where the Nelsons waited. "Any of them look familiar?"

They both shook their heads.

"No one stands out from the others." Mr. Nelson sighed. "Put a mask on any of them and they could be the one. I'm sorry."

So was Rowan. He'd hoped that they could lock Larson away.

How would the man retaliate? Would he go after him, the Larsons, or both?

"Is there a place the two of you can go other than your house? Somewhere out of town?"

"My mother's." Mrs. Nelson's eyes widened. "You think he'll come back?"

"It's possible."

Mr. Nelson put his arm around his wife. "We'll go stay at her mother's. Once the house is cleaned, I'm putting it on the market. I'm not staying in a town where a madman walks free."

Rowan didn't blame them. All he could do was vow to stop Larson before anyone else suffered.

Chapter Thirteen

Shiloh spent another restless night tossing and turning about whether or not she should risk breaking into Duke's house. The man wouldn't be stupid enough to keep evidence he'd committed the crime, right? Was she willing to take that chance?

Of course, she didn't want to be arrested and lose her job. She'd already let the other teachers know she would be taking a day off. What if she simply walked past Duke's house and see what happened?

Maybe he was home. Maybe he'd invite her in. Would she go? Absolutely not. No way would she be in his house with him alone. So, what then? Her mind spun so fast she got dizzy. Her breath came in gasps. It had been a long time since she'd had an anxiety attack.

Peanut whined and crawled closer, shoving her nose into Shiloh's armpit. Her breath tickled, and Shiloh giggled. "You're the best medicine, you silly dog." She wrapped her arms around the dog's neck and let her worries subside.

When the day had righted itself, she climbed from bed and put on comfortable clothes suitable for an early morning walk. Since autumn wasn't far off, the mornings had started to carry a slight chill, and the leaves displayed a touch of red and gold. Shiloh remembered fall in Misty Hollow as being beautiful. She called for the dog. "Do you feel like a long walk across the bridge or a short one where we drive into town?"

Peanut's ears perked up.

"Long walk it is." The exercise would do them both good.

She clipped a leash to the dog's collar. Poop bags and a collapsible bowl hung from the leash. Grabbing a water bottle, Shiloh set the alarm and closed the front door behind her. With a deep breath of the crisp morning air, Shiloh headed up the road, diverting her glance from the Nelson house. She didn't need to be reminded of what had happened there. That brutal act was why she'd set out this morning.

She paused on the bridge over Misty Creek and stared down at the water rushing under them. How many times had she sat there, legs dangling over the side, wishing to be somewhere else? Now, here she was, back by choice. "Life can be funny, Peanut."

They continued into town. Some folks waved as they drove past; others stared. She shrugged, having gotten used to the scrutiny fifteen years ago.

Did Duke live in the same house? That was a question that should have been answered before heading out on this crazy quest.

Shiloh passed the garage first, relieved to see his van in the lot, but there was no sign of Duke. She turned and headed to the neighborhood where the development people with money lived. Her stomach growled, reminding her she'd left without breakfast, so she made a detour to the diner.

Not seeing Rowan's car, she led Peanut to a table for two under an oak tree. She ordered biscuits and gravy and settled back to watch the cars drive past, some pulling into the lot. Her eyes narrowed at the sight of Duke's van, then she released the breath she'd been holding when he drove past without spotting her.

Rowan pulled into a spot. When he exited his car, he strode her way, a big smile on his face. "Playing hooky?"

"Sure am. I thought I'd take a day for a long walk, then maybe an afternoon nap." She returned his smile. "Then, breakfast sounded good."

"Breakfast always sounds good." He ordered pancakes and sausage when the server arrived. "And lots of coffee."

"Late night?"

He nodded. "Rachel kept me up complaining of her stomach. Then she threw up and felt better. I don't know where she got all that red licorice she consumed, but I don't think she'll be a glutton for a good long while."

Shiloh laughed. "Kids are never boring."

"That's for sure." He folded his arms on the table. "You okay?"

"Not sleeping as well as I'd like, but I'll be fine." As soon as the visions of the Nelsons stopped plaguing her. "Taking a day off to take a long walk will help." If nothing else, it would tire her out.

"Have you run across Duke?"

She frowned. "He worked at the school yesterday and was scheduled for today. That was another reason not to go in. There's a rumor he started that the two of us are dating."

"Really? He doesn't seem your type." His eyes twinkled.

"Very funny." She decided not to let him know about Duke's threats. There wasn't anything he could do about them. She declined his offer to pay for their food. When they finished eating, she looped Peanut's leash around her wrist and set off in the direction she'd previously been headed.

The mailbox in front of the yellow Victorian still read Larson. Since the name and house number were freshly painted, she could safely assume Duke had inherited his family home.

She gripped the iron bars of the gate that hadn't been there when they were teenagers. This prevented her entrance better than anything. Duke's security made up her mind for her—she wasn't going in.

~

What in the world was Shiloh doing staring through Larson's gate?

Rowan pulled up to the curb and rolled down the passenger window. "What are you doing?"

She gasped and spun around. "You scared me."

"Would that be because you're up to something you shouldn't be?"

"Like what?" Her wide-eyed innocent look didn't convince him.

He wiggled his fingers for her to come closer. "Why are you in front of Larson's house? Are you inviting trouble?"

She sighed. "I'm trying to find evidence of him being behind the attack on the Nelsons. I didn't expect a security gate."

"Were you going to trespass and break and enter?"

"What?"

"You heard me." He shoved open his door and joined her on the sidewalk. "You were contemplating breaking the law, am I right?"

She raised her nose in the air. "'Contemplating' being the magic word. I haven't committed a crime."

"Yet." His blood boiled. What did she think would happen if Duke caught her? "Do you realize how dangerous it is simply by being on this street?"

"I can't run scared all my life. I want him locked up, and I intend to find something on him that will do that."

"Leave that to law enforcement. To me. I will find something." Rowan rested his hands on her shoulders. "Trust me, Shiloh."

"I do, but it's taking so long."

He pulled her against his chest. Her hair smelled fresh and clean with a hint of floral. Closing his eyes, he took a deep breath.

"Listen, I want whatever I find to stick. I don't want to risk him walking free when I do make an arrest. Do you understand?" His heart almost stopped when he'd spotted her so close to Larson's property. The man wouldn't be pleased if she trespassed. He might have even thought she was coming on to him. Duke's moves on her would have increased, which would be dangerous.

She gave a muffled yes against his chest.

"Promise?"

"Ugh." She glared up at him. "Fine. I promise."

His gaze landed on her lips. What would she do if he kissed her?

Her eyes softened, giving him hope that she'd be

receptive to the idea.

The whine of the iron gate swinging open halted him. With an inward groan, he stepped back and faced the gate.

Larson, his face dark, marched toward them. "May I ask what the two of you are doing here?" His gaze landed on Shiloh.

She moved closer to Rowan causing Larson's face to turn the color of eggplant. "I was walking my dog, seeing all the changes in Misty Hollow, and ended up here. Beautiful gate."

"I saw Shiloh walking and stopped to say hello." Rowan forced a smile.

Larson glared his way. "By hugging on the sidewalk where anyone can see? What will people think to see my girl getting so close to another man?"

"I'm not your girl." Shiloh practically growled the words.

"Oh, my dear. You are sorely mistaken. Please take care in the future. I have a reputation to uphold."

"Not a very good one."

He spun back to face her. "Watch it, Shiloh."

"Let's go. I'll give you a ride home." Rowan needed to defuse the situation and fast. He opened the car door. "Get in, Shiloh."

She huffed and climbed in the passenger seat while Rowan put Peanut in back.

"You look like Rachel when she's in trouble."

"Am I in trouble?" She cut him a sideways glance.

"Not yet." He pulled away from the curb and left Larson watching after them.

"He won't like that you gave me a ride after he warned you to stay away." She clicked her seatbelt into place.

"Nope, but I wasn't going to leave you there."

They drove the rest of the way in silence. Rowan stopped in front of Shiloh's house, but she stayed in the car. After a few seconds, she turned to him.

"Were you going to kiss me back there?"

"I really, really wanted to. Would you have minded?"

"No, I think I would've like it." Her lips curled up.

He cupped the back of her head and pulled her close. "Let's make both of us happy then." Rowan kissed her softly at first, knowing there would be no going back after the kiss. Then, the kiss deepened as she made a soft sound in her throat and leaned closer. This was everything he'd dreamed of and more.

~

On Duke's quick trip home to retrieve a tool he'd left, the last thing he expected to see on his security camera was Shiloh in the arms of the deputy. Now, they kissed, completely disregarding his order to stay away from each other.

Duke stormed back to where he'd left his van, blood boiling like a volcano, and sped back to the garage. He had work to do, a living to make. The last thing he needed was a strong-headed woman that needed to be put in her place.

He kicked the tire of a car needing repairs and stalked into his office. Slamming the door, he dropped into his desk, cupping his head with his hands. What could he do to make her see reason?

The dog? Not something he wanted to do. He'd never hurt a dog or a small child. But...he straightened...Shiloh didn't know that. She thought of him as a monster.

So would the rest of the townsfolk if she didn't stop keeping him at arm's length. Most of them thought she wanted him. Why didn't she? Didn't that night mean anything to her? No one since then had meant as much as she did. Why couldn't she see his devotion?

Ugh. He beat his fists against his head, then bolted to his feet. Work, then plans. A gift, maybe. A kitten? Jewelry? Both?

He didn't need to decide right then. Shiloh wasn't going anywhere, and neither was he.
But he couldn't say the same for the deputy.

Chapter Fourteen

Crime-scene cleaners had come and gone and now, in a week's time, a for-sale sign sat in the Nelsons' yard. Shiloh sighed and shook her head. How many more people would move away before Duke was stopped?

She had to be careful not to make close friends or speak to anyone about him. Shiloh had managed to keep Rowan at arm's length for his safety and hers, but she couldn't stop thinking about that kiss. Did he think about it too? Now was not the time for romance. Not until this was over. She'd do well to remember that fact.

She parked in her usual spot at the school and headed to an early morning meeting with the other two fifth-grade teachers. Her mouth fell open at the sight of Melinda's black eye. "What happened?"

"Ran into a door in the middle of the night." She avoided Shiloh's gaze.

"Did Duke do that? If so, you need to report it to the sheriff." She dropped her bag on the table with a thunk. "Enough is enough, Melinda."

"Mind your own business." She crossed her arms and glared.

"I'm only trying to—"

"Well, don't. Anything bad that happens is all your fault. You shouldn't have come back."

Shiloh's heart dropped. Everything was always laid on her shoulders. When would she be able to leave it all behind and show the townsfolk who the real Shiloh was? She'd almost started to believe that the old prejudices were dying away. "Have it your way."

"Thanks. I will."

Susan entered Melinda's class. Bright red stained her cheeks once she saw Melinda's face. She shook her head and clamped her lips together.

"I think the three of us should go to the sheriff about what Duke did to us." What he was still doing to her. Shiloh refused to be deterred. "Deputy Reynolds will help us."

"And what?" Melinda's eyes flashed. "Have the town treat us the way they treat you? No, thanks. If you say anything, I'll deny it."

Shiloh glanced at Susan who shook her head. "Fine. I'll take care of things myself." She plopped into a chair. "Let's get this meeting over with." Any hopes of these two women being allies, maybe even friends, died away.

They spent the next forty-five minutes adjusting lesson plans and preparing for state testing. When they finished, Shiloh gathered her things and hurried from the room to the sanctuary of her own classroom.

Why didn't they want Duke stopped? They need to come forward about the abuse. It would take too long for her to do it without them. She folded her arms on the desk and rested her head on them. Most likely, there were more victims, but she didn't know who they were. Somehow, she needed to convince Susan and Melinda to help. Maybe Rowan would talk to them.

It would probably make them madder than they already were, but she was growing desperate. A time bomb was suspended over her head, ready to go off at any time, and she was right in the blast zone.

She sent him a text asking him to meet her in the school cafeteria for lunch if he was available. He responded within a couple of minutes to say he'd be there.

Good. Shiloh headed outside to collect her students wondering how she could keep the news of Rowan stopping by from Duke. Very little got past the residents of small towns.

Rowan was waiting for her inside the cafeteria at lunch time. "You rang?" He gave her a smile that sent her heart flipping.

"Let's grab our food and eat in my room. I need your help."

His smile faded. "All right."

They bypassed the students in line and filled their plates from the teachers' salad bar. Rowan added a burger and fries before following her to her room. He squeezed his bulk onto a student's chair. "What's up?"

"Don't you want to eat first?" She arched a brow.

"I can eat while you talk." He picked up the burger.

"Okay. I want you to speak to Susan Snodgrass and Melinda Larson, the other fifth-grade teachers, about Duke abusing them." She set her jaw.

He set the burger down. "Them too?"

She nodded.

"You're positive?"

"We've made mention of it, the three of us.

Melinda has a black eye today, and I think Duke gave it to her because he's mad about me and you, and she was the closest to his fist." Not that there really was a her and him.

The look on Rowan's face would spear a wild boar. He exhaled heavily and stared at the Styrofoam plate in front of him. After several tense seconds, he raised his head. "I'll speak with them."

"What if they won't talk to you? They've already told me they'd deny any abuse." She clutched her plastic spork so hard it cracked.

"I'll let them know that if and when he's taken to court, they'll be subpoenaed. They'd have to talk then." He ate like a starving man. "I'll look for them now. Thank you for letting me know." When he'd finished, he dropped his plate in the garbage. "Stay safe, Shiloh. I can't be everywhere at once. You need to help me keep you safe."

She wasn't sure she was up to the task. What kind of risks was she willing to take to put Duke away?

~

Rowan wanted to strangle Duke more than he'd ever wanted to hurt anyone before. The man wasn't going to get away with his crimes this time. Women were not to be used and tossed aside. He'd cherished his late wife and intended to cherish Shiloh if she'd let him once this was all over. He wanted his daughter to know how a woman should be treated, and he believed in leading by example.

He found Susan Snodgrass leading her students to her room. "Ma'am, I'd like a moment of your time, please."

She sighed, her expression letting him know she

knew what he wanted, and told her students to go sit down and read until she came in. Once the door closed behind them, she faced Rowan. "Make it quick, Deputy. I've a job to do."

"So do I, ma'am." He kept his expression as impassive as possible, a look he'd perfected during his years as a deputy.

She crossed her arms, an unfriendly expression on her face. "Well?"

"Has Duke Larson ever assaulted you?" No sense in beating around the bush. "In the past or recently?"

At first, she didn't appear as if she would respond. "Why are you digging, Deputy? You're stirring a fire that doesn't need to be stirred."

"Is that an affirmative answer, Ms. Snodgrass?"

"I'm not affirming anything." She crossed her arms. "I'm not replying at all. Just leave it alone."

"Why is the town still afraid? Duke is the last of his immediate family. The Larsons don't have the power they once had."

"You're fairly new to Misty Hollow, Deputy Reynolds. You have no idea what you're talking about."

He arched a brow. "Really? Why don't you fill me in on how one man can hold a town hostage."

She glanced around as if someone would hear. "Please. Leave it alone."

"I wouldn't be doing my job."

Shaking her head, she reached for the door handle to her class. "You're keeping me from my job."

"If you reach the point where you want to talk, I'm here." He waited for her to enter her room before heading to the class of Melinda Larson.

She gave him a death glare when he stepped into her classroom. "Can I help you?"

"I certainly hope so. Can you step into the hall?"

The class oohed. One boy said she was in trouble now.

Rowan smiled and shook his head. "I only have a question. Miss Larson is not in trouble."

She brushed past him without glancing up. In the hall, she whipped around. "I have nothing to say."

"About what?" He arched a brow. "I haven't asked you anything yet."

"Fine. What do you want to know?"

"How'd you get the black eye?"

"Door."

"Did Duke Larson hit you?"

"I told you I ran into a door." Her gaze shifted to the left, a sure sign she lied.

"Has he assaulted you recently or in the past?"

"He's my cousin."

"That doesn't answer my question."

"Why are you asking me this?" Her gaze flicked back to his, then shifted over his shoulder.

"Ma'am, if he is ever brought to trial over allegations of abuse or molestation, you and Miss Snodgrass will be subpoenaed. Wouldn't you like to bring an end to this?" He glanced back to see what had made her pale.

Duke Larson, a box of fluorescent light bulbs over his shoulder, strode past the end of the hall. He gave a sarcastic salute as he passed.

"Please." Her words barely came above a whisper. "Leave me alone. You'll only make it worse."

"This sheriff's department can keep you safe."

"Like they'll keep Shiloh safe? No thanks."

"You've heard of threats against her?" His blood chilled. An icy fist clenched his heart.

"Everyone knows he won't stop until he gets what he wants. What he wants is Shiloh."

"Why does he care so much?"

"Because she's the one who got away."

"Please call me if you're threatened again." He handed her a business card. "Night or day. Don't let him treat you this way."

She took the card and slipped it into the pocket of her slacks. "What way?"

He stifled a sigh. "Thank you for your time. Have a good day." He turned and went in search of Larson.

~

Duke slid a bulb into place. What was that no-good deputy doing at the school? Had Shiloh called him? Neither of them could take a hint, apparently. He'd been working on a plan to show them how serious he was, but it wasn't the time to implement it. He still held onto hope that Shiloh would come around. "Sugar rather than vinegar," his grandmother always said, but he wasn't finished using sugar. He climbed from the ladder to see the deputy standing in the doorway of the copy room. "What do you want?"

"Did you spend some time with Melinda Larson last night?"

"No." He lifted the box of bulbs. "Why would you think that? Did she say something?"

"The opposite in fact."

Good. His cousin knew to keep her mouth shut if she knew what was good for her. "I was home watching TV until bedtime. I've been working hard the last few days."

The deputy simply kept his stony gaze on him.

Worry trickled through him. Did Reynolds know more than he was letting on? Had Melinda said something without actually saying the words? Duke needed to be more careful in the future. He shouldn't let his anger get control of him. Especially when it meant leaving marks where people could see them.

When had he developed such a taste for power over people? Since birth, most likely. His mother had definitely been frightened of his father, and his grandmother of his grandfather. Power was in his blood, and this town knew it.

"What's going through that evil mind of yours, Larson?"

"I'm wondering when you're going to leave so I can finish this and get to the garage."

Reynolds didn't look convinced. "Since I don't have any proof you gave Miss Larson that black eye, I'm going to say one thing. Make sure you don't. Not her, not any woman in this town or any other. Got it?"

Duke smirked. "Sure thing, Deputy. I know my place." It would do the other man well to know his. Someday. Someday, Duke would put the deputy in his place and derive great pleasure in doing so.

The other man's gaze dropped to Duke's feet. No worries. He'd cleaned the blood off his boot right after Shiloh noticed.

Chapter Fifteen

The week had passed with nothing worse than Shiloh's co-teachers ignoring her. Shiloh had started eating alone in her room at lunch. She tried to tell herself she didn't care, but it was a lie. Still, bringing all this to the light would only help rid this town of its resident, arrogant, entitled, last-male-standing Larson. Also, not true. There were a few cousins spread across the country, but they'd left Misty Hollow a long time ago and hadn't shown the same pure meanness Duke and his father had.

She grabbed Peanut's leash but didn't clip it on her collar. Since they were headed into the woods, she'd only attach it if she felt a need to. "Let me show you a place that's very special to me, girl."

The sun warmed the day. Probably one of the few remaining days before the chill of fall settled in for good. Shiloh intended to enjoy it. She grabbed a backpack from the kitchen table and settled it across her back before going outside. After setting the alarm, she headed for the thick stand of woods behind her house.

The forest was one of the reasons her grandfather

had bought the house. After losing all his own land in a poker deal, he'd purchased this little shack because the government land behind it made him feel a bit more like he still owned an acreage.

He and her father had shot many a deer and squirrel among those trees. Not Shiloh. She'd made herself a few hidey holes for when her parents were fighting. One of them, she'd never shown to another living soul. Now, she intended to share the place with her dog.

They walked maybe a football field away from the house. Shiloh stood where she thought the hiding place was and turned in a slow circle. Things looked a lot different after fifteen years.

Ivy had covered some of the trees. Some poison, some not. A couple of boulders had slid down the mountain. Had they covered the entrance?

She took a flashlight from the backpack and moved to where the mountain started to rise to touch the sky. About ten feet up there had been…she saw it and smiled. Unless a person knew it was there, they'd never guess the dark shadow behind some mulberry bushes was a small cave.

Shiloh started to climb, hoping an animal hadn't claimed the place for its own. "Check it out, Peanut." She lifted some branches. "See if it's safe."

The dog, nose to the ground, entered the cave. When no growls or barks emanated, Shiloh followed.

The cave smelled of dampness and rich Ozark clay. The old quilt she'd left in there remained, soiled with a few holes, but amazingly intact. An old battery-operated lantern lay on its side.

Shiloh bent and picked up a moldy edition of *Black*

Stallion. She'd loved that book as a little girl. Somewhere at the house, she'd hidden a letter and a photo from Walter Farley, having written him in the fourth grade as part of a school assignment.

"What do you think? It's the Ritz Carlton, right?" She laughed and patted the dog's head. "This little place holds so many memories."

A small pile of bones showed evidence an animal had spent some time there. The lack of fresh footprints showed it hadn't been recent.

Mindless of dirtying her jeans, Shiloh sat on the ground and picked up a stick she had used to poke the embers of a small fire during the colder months. She leaned against the dirt wall. This place had been her sanctuary.

Peanut plopped next to her and laid her head on Shiloh's thigh. She sighed and stared up at her, complete devotion shining from her dark eyes.

"I sure hope a man looks at me someday with as much love in his eyes as you do." She placed her hand on the dog's head and let the memories flood her.

No longer the frightened child, she refused to become a scared woman. Duke hadn't been seen around the house in weeks. He'd finished his work at the school. Unless she ran into him in town or at the diner, she most likely wouldn't see him. The man would figure out she didn't plan on going out with him. She still planned on seeking justice for what he'd done to her and the others, though. Even if it elicited a reaction from the man.

When she started to shiver from sitting on the damp ground, she stood. "Let's go home. We'll bring more blankets and a new lantern, Peanut. Make this our special place again. Can you imagine a nap here? Surrounded by the wonders of nature? I can, and it looks divine. A place to get away from the craziness of the world." She listened to the silence, then smiled and ducked back into the warmth of the blanket. Shiloh took her time heading back to the house. She spotted Rowan on her back deck the minute she cleared the trees. The rigidness of his body was visible as she approached. "Well, howdy."

"Hi." He grinned. "Rachel wanted to play with Peanut, so I picked up a pizza and brought it over just in case you were home."

"I'm always home."

"No, we've been here half an hour."

She ignored the question in his eyes. "Not far. Worried?"

"A little." His grin widened. "Is that okay?"

She nodded, pleased that she had someone to worry about her. Maybe someday, she'd show him her special place.

~

Rowan had been more than a little worried, if he were honest. After fifteen minutes of no sight of her or Peanut, he'd checked the garage. Seeing her car there had sent his heart racing. Only after the initial panic had he figured out she must have taken a walk into the woods. The alarm had been set after all.

He should have her change the code, but he liked knowing he could check on her at any time. Stalker much, Rowan? "Does it bother you that I let myself in?"

Her brow furrowed. "You know? It really doesn't." Her gaze locked with his. "It seems…normal."

It did, strange enough. His heart warmed, and he opened the door for her. It did feel normal. He called Rachel away from the television to eat. The three gathered around the kitchen table like family. Like the family he'd once had—something he was ready for again. With Shiloh, possibly? It was definitely something he wanted to explore. "Would you like to go on a date with me sometime?" The words blurted out.

From the expression on her face, she hadn't expected the question any more than he'd expected asking it. "Sure." Her gaze flicked to where Rachel sat engrossed in a cartoon.

"She'll be happy." Rowan smiled. "How about Friday night? We'll get out of Misty Hollow. Eat at a nice place in Langley. Do you like Japanese?"

She nodded. "There aren't many foods I don't like." Her cheeks had turned a cute shade of pink, letting him see the shy young girl she'd once been.

"Great. I'll pick you up at five-thirty. That way I can be back before Rachel's bedtime."

"You're a good father, Rowan." Her tone sounded wistful as she took paper plates from the top of the refrigerator. "Not every little girl has a father like you."

"What was yours like?"

She gave a one-shoulder shrug. "Drank a lot. Kept a job, barely. Hit Mom some. I spent a lot of time alone in the woods." She handed him a plate. "That's where I was when you arrived. Visiting old, special places."

"Maybe you'll show me sometime."

A soft smile graced her lips. "Maybe."

"Dad?" Rachel had gotten up from the sofa and now stared out the front door.

"Yeah, sweetie?"

"Sasquatch is outside again. He's walking around that house at the top of the hill."

"That's probably Mr. Nelson."

She shook her head. "He's fuzzy."

Rowan frowned at Shiloh, then moved to the window. The form of a man wearing something "fuzzy" slipped around the corner of the Nelson home.

"Here." Shiloh handed him a pair of binoculars. At his questioning look, she shrugged again. "I like to watch birds."

"Do you know where the preserve is? You'd enjoy it there." He lifted the binoculars to his eyes.

The man wore a camouflage outfit, strips of material made out to look like leaves. The fact he didn't want to be recognized meant he was up to no good.

Rowan handed the binoculars back to Shiloh. "Keep Rachel here." He hurried out the door and retrieved his service weapon from the glove compartment of his car. Slipping into the trees lining the road, he headed up the hill, searching for a vehicle. So far, nothing. No Larson construction van or the man's truck. Of course, that didn't mean anything. There were roads through the trees where someone could park out of sight.

He slowed as he approached the house. The camouflaged man moved back into sight but was still too far away for Rowan to make himself known. The trespasser would have too much time to escape.

Increasing his pace, Rowan stepped from the trees and sprinted for the house. The man froze and glanced back revealing a dark-face mask. "Stop. Deputy!"

The man fired a weapon.

Rowan dove into a bush. When he popped up to

return fire, the man had hidden. The rattle of something behind the house alerted him to the fact the man hadn't fled.

His palm sweated around the butt of his weapon. He took a deep breath and slowly emerged from his hiding place. *God, don't let me get shot.* He couldn't leave Rachel without a father. Strange how times like this made him question his career choice. Leaving his daughter an orphan was a real possibility.

Another shot dug into the ground near his feet. He skirted the house, the rough siding pulling at the sleeves of his tee-shirt. He glanced toward Shiloh's house.

She stood on the porch, the red of her shirt a direct contrast to the white of the house. Shaking his head and ushering another prayer that she wouldn't get caught in the crossfire, he continued his pursuit. The other house couldn't be hit without a sniper rifle, and he doubted the man he sought had one, or he'd have been dead the moment he stepped from Shiloh's front door.
Still, he didn't like her out in the open.

Back against the wall, he peered around the corner. Nobody…wait. He caught sight of the man fleeing into the woods behind the house. Rowan had been correct in assuming he'd parked on a back road.

Now that the man fled, he darted after him, not as worried about catching a bullet. Hard to run and hit a target behind.

Whoever he chased seemed to be in better shape than he was. Rowan's breaths came in gasps, his thighs burned. He'd been slack in going to the gym and regretted it big time. He burst from the trees onto a logging road almost completely overgrown with weeds. A rusty truck kicked up rocks as the driver stepped on the gas.

Rowan aimed for the tires and fired his gun. Bam, bam, bam. One bullet hit its target, but the truck kept going.

So close. He'd been a hair from proving Larson behind it all. If only he'd been able to see the man's face.

Why was he snooping around the Nelson home? A cleaning team had already been in the house after CSI finished.

He turned back and did a slow walk around the perimeter of the house. Other than the print of a work boot which most men in the town wore, he didn't see anything of interest.

Something glinted in the grass, half hidden under fallen leaves.

Rowan moved the leaves with his foot.

A bloody knife.

He'd bet anything that he'd found the knife used on the Nelsons. The culprit had dropped it. Why? Had his work been interrupted? Was that why the Nelsons still lived? Who would have come?

He glanced up and down the road. Shiloh hadn't been home. Something had made the man drop the knife. That's what he'd come back to find. If not for the leaves, Rowan wouldn't have found the weapon. He smiled and called the sheriff's office, then texted Shiloh and asked if she knew of anyone who might have come to her house on that date.

"I received a package. New clothes."

His smile widened. A simple delivery van had interrupted that day. He moved to the front porch and glanced around to see whether the Nelsons had a package. Wedged between the wall and a heavy planter was a white padded envelope.

Rowan had someone else to question.

Chapter Sixteen

Another peaceful week with no trouble from Duke. The iciness of her coworkers had subsided to a chill.

To end the week, she had a date with Rowan. A real date. The first date she'd had in longer than she cared to admit. A miracle, really, that she'd let Rowan slip through a crevice in the wall she'd erected around her. Since leaving Misty Hollow, she'd mostly kept men at an arm's length. Her father hadn't been a good man to model anyone by. Neither was Duke.

But Rowan...he was different. Kind, strong, and a good father. She could see herself wanting to know him better. Tonight, with no Rachel chattering nonstop, she had that chance.

Hair in an updo, a dress that made her blue eyes pop, a touch of makeup, and she stood at the front door waiting. She had finished early, not that Rowan was late.

A shadow moved in the trees behind the garage. Shiloh narrowed her eyes and focused on the spot. She thought she saw movement again, but whatever it was didn't show once Rowan pulled in front of her house. If not for "Sasquatch," she'd have thought nothing of it.

"Wow." Rowan's face lit up with appreciation. "You always look nice, but tonight you're spectacular."

Her face warmed. "You don't look so bad yourself." In fact, the form-fitting, button-down shirt and dark pants made him good enough to eat.

"My mother always said I cleaned up nice." The corner of his mouth quirked. "Ready?"

"Yes." She set the alarm, patted Peanut, then pulled the door closed behind her.

"Everything good this week?" He opened the passenger-side door.

"So far." She smiled. Did she dare hope Duke had given up?

Once they were on the Interstate, she asked, "Do you have any family?"

"No, my parents were gone before Rachel was born. My wife's parents moved to California after her death.

"They don't see Rachel?" She couldn't imagine.

"They said it hurt too much. It doesn't make sense to me. Their granddaughter is a mini version of Rose. I'd think it would be a bit like having their daughter back, but since there's nothing I can do about it, I'll let it be."

"Maybe someday, they'll come around."

"Maybe."

"Siblings?"

"A sister teaching in the Middle East."

"I guess you know I'm an only child." She tilted her head.

"Yep. I asked about you when you arrived in town, and this whole thing with Duke started."

"So, you know I'm from the wrong side of the

bridge. At least, I used to be. Things have improved since I left." She stared out the window.

New homes, more cleared fields, yes, a lot of things had changed in the last fifteen years. Most of it good. She turned and studied his profile. Her heart hoped he would be the best of the good. It was time for her to have more than just herself.

"What are you thinking?" He arched a brow.

She laughed, feeling braver than ever. "I was thinking how handsome you are."

"Aw, shucks."

"I bet you've been told that before."

"A time or two." He reached over and took her hand. "I don't hold a candle to you, sweetheart."

The endearment settled over her like a child's favorite blanket. The flush returned to her cheeks as he lifted her hand to his lips.

A few minutes later, he parked in front of a Japanese restaurant where they grilled the food in front of the patrons. Shiloh waited for him to open her door for her, then slipped her hand in his so he could help her from the car. She could get used to this kind of attention from a man.

Her mind spun down ridiculous paths. Could he love another woman as much as he seemed to have loved his first wife? A lot of people remarried and led a happy, fulfilled life, right?

A frown furrowed between his eyes, and she smiled to show everything was fine. He returned her smile and tucked her hand in the crook of his arm.

A car backfired.

Rowan shoved her behind him, then laughed when he realized no danger existed. "Sorry."

She faced him, staring into his eyes. "I'm safe here with you."

He leaned his forehead against hers. "I can't save you from a bullet."

"Duke doesn't want me dead." She stepped back and cupped his cheek. "Let's go inside so you'll feel better."

~

Rowan couldn't believe he'd mistaken a car's backfire for a gunshot. He stifled a groan as he placed a hand on the small of Shiloh's back and guided her into the restaurant. He was there to protect her, and she ended up calming him. This case was getting to him. "Two, please." He forced a smile at the hostess who led them to a corner table.

"Are you okay?" Shiloh glanced up at him as he held out her chair for her.

"Yeah. Sorry about being so jumpy." He sat in a chair facing the door. "I..." He slumped, his gaze on hers. "What if I can't keep you safe? I failed my wife. What makes me think I can save you?"

"This is different, Rowan." She reached over and put a hand on his. "She died of cancer. This isn't an unseen disease. This is a flesh-and-blood man. I have complete confidence in you."

If only he had the same confidence. He'd never faltered before on the job, but his growing feelings for Shiloh left him fearful of failure. How had a simple case of keeping an eye on someone threatened by another become something so much more?

A server in black pants and a white blouse handed them menus, pulling him from his thoughts. "I'll be back in a few minutes." She smiled and left them.

Shiloh laughed. "No ordering the special tonight."

"No." He smiled. "I'll have to venture out and try something new."

By the time their server returned, he'd decided on a steak while Shiloh ordered salmon. He handed their menus back and reached for his water glass as he let his gaze roam over those in the restaurant.

No one seemed to be paying them any undue attention. Shiloh seemed relaxed. It would be a good evening. "How would you feel about a walk this evening?"

She took a drink of her water. "Here in Langley?"

"No. Back home. We could stroll down Main Street or head to the lake. There won't be many mild nights left before it's too cold."

"I'd prefer the lake, please. Fewer disapproving stares."

He rested his hand of hers. "I wish I could take all that away from you."

A shadow crossed over her features. "I'm used to it."

"No one should be used to poor treatment." He took her hand in his, entwining their fingers. "You're a good woman, Shiloh. People will realize that in time. Especially after teaching their children for a year."

"I hope so."

The rest of supper was spent with humorous stories of the children in her class and the recent antics of Rachel who had not been happy to be left behind for her father's date.. His daughter seemed to think she should go with them every time.

At the lake, Shiloh's steps faltered as they headed down the walking path. "This is where I saw the rose petals."

"Do you still believe they were left there as a romantic gesture for someone else?" He hadn't heard of any recent engagements in town, but that wasn't to say there hadn't been one. He entwined their fingers, enjoying the feel of her smaller hand in his.

A slight breeze blew a few stray strands of hair around her face, and she shivered. The moon cast diamonds on the water's surface. "I left my sweater in your car," she said.

He glanced back, relieved he could see his vehicle. "Wait here." Rowan jogged to the car and retrieved her sweater, returning as fast as possible. He definitely didn't want to leave her alone in the dark any longer than necessary.

"Thank you." She slipped her arms through the sleeves. "It's a beautiful night."

He gazed into eyes shining by moonlight. "Yes." He cupped her face. "I'm going to kiss you now, Shiloh."

Her lips parted slightly. He lowered his head and claimed her lips. A soft sigh brushed across his as she returned the kiss. Soft, sweet, and perfect for such a romantic evening.

A splash jerked them apart.

Rowan studied the bank for signs of movement.

"What is it?" Shiloh whispered, staying close to his side.

"An animal most likely." But, said animal had yet to show itself. He wanted to go check, but he didn't want to put Shiloh into possible danger or leave her behind.

"I'd like to go back now, please."

"Okay." He gripped her hand and headed quickly back to the car. The hair on the back of his neck stood at attention. His gut instinct told him they weren't alone out there.

~

Clumsy idiot. Duke stared through a low-hanging branch. Tripping and sending that rock tumbling into the water had almost given him away.

When he'd spotted them driving through town and followed them, he hadn't expected a romantic liaison at the lake. His hands curled into fists. Why didn't anyone take his threats seriously?

He melted into the shadows. Tomorrow, they'd see he meant business.

Once the taillights of the deputy's car disappeared out of sight, Duke jogged to where he'd left his van behind some thick bushes. No need to follow them. He knew exactly where they'd be going. Back to Shiloh's house for another kiss.

Sure enough, the two locked lips on her porch. His fingers curled around the steering wheel as he wished for his rifle so he could rid the world of the deputy. If he wasn't around, Shiloh would turn to him for consolation.

After rejecting her for a while to make her pay for her betrayal, he'd then offer a consoling shoulder. Yep, getting rid of the deputy was the key.

How, though? Right now, if the deputy died, Duke would be the primary suspect. The deputy was well liked around town, but so was he. However, the sheriff's department was another story. Whenever he ran across a deputy or the sheriff, he received stony glances instead of smiles.

What kind of rumors had Reynolds spread about him? This was Duke's town, and he had no intention of letting it go.

As the deputy headed back to his car, Duke turned and drove away. He didn't need to be seen watching them.

The incident when he'd returned to find his knife had been too close. His heart had almost stopped when the deputy stumbled across it.

Would they find out the knife was custom made? If so, they'd know exactly who it belonged to. That wouldn't do at all. Somehow, he needed to retrieve that knife.

Who could he bribe at the department to grab it out of the evidence room? Not the woman deputy. She looked at him as if he were scum. The other man? The receptionist? If he could find something they cared enough about and threatened them, they'd be more than happy to do as he asked.

Whistling now that he had solid plans, Duke headed home to get a good night's sleep. The next few days promised to be very busy.

He headed to Melinda's to work off some frustration.

Chapter Seventeen

Duke stood, back plastered against the deputy's house, and waited for the prime moment he could snip the brake lines without being seen. Why did people want to live surrounded by neighbors anyway? He preferred his nearest neighbor to be more than an arm's length away.

A curtain twitched across the street. Some Nosy Nelly was bound to call the deputy. He cursed and returned to his vehicle before someone recognized him.

In the driver's seat of his van, he watched Reynolds and his little girl climb into the car. Since it wasn't a school day, they were probably heading to the diner to have breakfast with Shiloh as they usually did on the weekend. He slammed his palm against the steering wheel. It ought to be him eating breakfast with her.

Duke followed, parking a few spots away from the deputy. He sent the man a death glare. The daughter scowled at him, then stuck out her tongue. Brat. When Shiloh and her dog arrived, Duke chose an outside table near them. He might as well make a nuisance of himself, and it wasn't against the law to sit close by. Maybe he'd figure out why Shiloh was so enamored with the deputy—learn some tips to win her over.

If it was because the man had a child, then Duke was out of luck. He most definitely never wanted to raise any child but his own. When Shiloh returned childless, he'd immediately imagined a child of theirs. A little boy just like him. All he needed now was Shiloh to feel the same, which meant getting rid of the deputy and stepping in to console her.

Now, he waited for the deputy to receive the call. Then, he'd take care of the brake lines.

~

Shiloh couldn't relax with Duke staring at them. "Can't you tell him to go away?"

"Unfortunately, he isn't breaking the law. Try and ignore him."

She narrowed her eyes at the other man who simply smiled. "Hard to do."

"You're a teacher. Surely, you know how to ignore unwanted behaviors." Rowan's mouth twitched.

"Of course, I can, but I don't expect to have to on the weekends." She returned his smile. "What's the special today?"

"Biscuits and chocolate gravy."

"Yum. That's what I'm having."

When their server, Dolly, arrived, Rowan ordered three specials before returning his attention to Shiloh. "Thank you again for a wonderful evening last night."

"I'm sorry I got spooked and cut it short." Embarrassment burned through her. She'd wondered at his jumping when a car backfired, and then she'd run like a frightened rabbit because of a splash in the lake.

"This whole thing with Larson has us both spooked." He placed his hand over hers. "I still enjoyed the date. There's no one I'd rather be spooked with."

"Silly." She laughed and straightened as Dolly placed their orders in front of them. A slice of bacon sat on the edge of the plate. "Thank you, Dolly."

Their server smiled. "Can't forget the dog."

Shiloh bit into a biscuit slathered with rich, thick chocolate. She closed her eyes in bliss and savored the flavor.

"If you don't stop looking like that, I'm going to kiss you right here in front of everyone."

"Do it, Daddy!"

Shiloh's eyes popped open to see both of the Reynolds grinning like loons. "It's very good." Embarrassed twice in one morning had to be a record even for her.

"You're cute when your face is all red."

"Would you shut up and eat?" She laughed and dug back into her breakfast. When she glanced at the table where Duke sat, he wasn't there.

"He left when your eyes were closed." Rowan's eyes twinkled. "Probably couldn't take the temptation."

"Stop it." Her face flushed again. Good grief. She acted like a teenage girl with a crush instead of a grown woman attracted to a handsome man.

"Want to go out again this Friday night?"

"Can I come?" Rachel glanced from him to Shiloh.

"No, sweetie. This is my and Shiloh's time."

"Oh, pooh." She crossed her arms and pouted.

"What are your plans for today?" Rowan dropped his napkin on his empty plate.

"Absolutely nothing except reading on my back deck. You?"

"I have some errands to run. Never seems to be

time during the week."

"I don't have a little girl to take up my time." She gave Rachel a one-armed hug. "How about a picnic on Sunday afternoon with all three of us?"

Rachel nodded. "Okay. Can I pick the place?"

"Sure."

Her forehead wrinkled. "How about your backyard?"

"Really?"

"It's pretty enough now that you planted flowers."

Shiloh glanced at Rowan. "Is that all right with you?"

"Absolutely." His phone buzzed on the table. He glanced at the screen, then pushed to his feet. "Do you mind watching Rachel for a few hours?"

"Sure. Is everything okay?"

"Melinda Larson is in the hospital. A broken arm and bruises. The sheriff is asking me to go question her. I shouldn't be gone long."

"Take as long as you need. Rachel and I will read on the deck. We'll have a great time." Poor Melinda. Shiloh didn't have to ask questions in order to know Duke had gotten heavy-handed with her last night. Maybe now, Melinda would talk.

~

Rowan parked in a spot reserved for law enforcement, then headed into Langley Hospital. The volunteer at the front desk directed him to Melinda's room on the second floor.

Bruises the color of eggplant marred her face. One eye looked nearly swollen shut. Her left arm wore a cast. Someone had beaten her badly.

"Hello, Miss Larson. Mind if I take a seat?"

She closed her eyes as if resigned. "Suit yourself."

"Can you tell me what happened?" He sat and pulled a small notepad from the pocket of his shirt.

"Car accident?"

"Really?" He arched a brow. "Where's the car now?"

"Towed." She glared with her one good eye.

"Did Duke Larson beat you?"

"I told you I had a car accident."

Why was she still covering for him? "If you'd be honest with me, I could help you."

"Empty promises." She turned her head away from him. "I'm tired. Please go."

He stifled a groan. If she'd just admit Larson did this, Rowan could arrest him. Lock him up for a night or two. He couldn't do anything if she refused to press charges. "I don't understand why you would cover up for someone who did this to you." He pushed to his feet. "If you should change your mind, please give me a call. If you were assaulted, even years ago, we could lock up the perpetrator. Think about how wonderful it would be if you no longer had to live in fear. One of these times, he might kill you."

Sobs followed him from the room. He took a deep breath and strode to the elevators. In his career, he'd met other domestic-abuse victims who refused to press charges, but he never could understand why.

He sat in his car for a few minutes trying to think of a way to persuade Melinda Larson to talk. If she would, then maybe Susan Snodgrass would come forward. With them and Shiloh, they could lock Larson up for a very long time.

With a sigh, he turned the key in the ignition and

headed back to Misty Hollow where Rachel and Shiloh awaited. Maybe in the future, they'd both be waiting for him at the end of the workday.

After Rose's death, he never thought he'd find another woman whom he'd consider spending his life with. Until Shiloh. His daughter already loved her, and Rowan was quickly heading in that direction. Yes, he'd like to come home each night to Shiloh.

With his thoughts on a possible future with Shiloh, the time passed quickly. He headed up Misty Mountain. In less than twenty minutes, he'd reach the valley and drive over the bridge.

Rowan slowed when a car pulled out of a side road. His gas pedal sank, but only slowed his car down. He'd have to ask a mechanic to take a look. Too bad the only mechanic in Misty Hollow happened to be Duke Larson—the last person he wanted touching his vehicle.

When he pressed the brake to go around a sharp curve, it became evident that the time for a mechanic had passed. The car swerved. Luckily, no one was coming from the opposite direction.

What wasn't so lucky was the fact the car picked up speed now as it headed into the valley. Rowan kept his senses alert, his grip light on the steering wheel, and scanned ahead of him for a small stand of bushes or saplings that could stop him without too much damage.

His tires squealed as he careened around another sharp curve. Trees rose on his right, a steep incline on his left. If he didn't find something soon, he'd have to use the side of the mountain to stop the speeding car.

He turned the wheel to the right. The car scraped along the rock face and protruding tree roots slowing him, but not enough. Another curve and the car sped up. How long could he keep going at that speed before crashing?

Praying another vehicle didn't meet him, he kept the car in the center of the road and fought to keep control. All he had to do was make it to the bottom of the mountain. Then, the car would eventually slow and stop.

"Come on, girl. Hold on. We've got this." Thank God for his defensive-driving skills, although he didn't think losing his brakes was exactly what the class had been for. His hands tightened in preparation for the next curve—a hairpin curve that almost made a person meet the back end of the car.

The wheels barely missed the cliff on his left as the car lifted on two tires, then settled so hard Rowan's teeth clattered. If he made it down alive, he'd kiss Shiloh so hard she couldn't breathe. Then, he'd wrap his arms around both her and his daughter and never let them go.

A yell escaped him at another curve, the car now rocketing toward the valley. A tree stubbornly clinging to the mountain wall on his right seemed his only recourse. The arrival of an oncoming truck made the decision for him.

His last thought before glass shattered, airbags deployed, and darkness overtook him was of Shiloh and his baby girl.

Chapter Eighteen

Rowan came to as someone shook and patted his shoulder. He groaned and peered through slitted eyelids. "What happened?"

"Dude, you came around that corner real fast and swerved into that tree. The ambulance is on its way. I couldn't get you out of the car on my own. You okay?" Now that he could see a bit better, he made out the worried face of a man in his late teens or early twenties.

"I...think so." He shoved the airbag away from his face and tried to move his legs. They were stuck for sure. At least he hoped they were stuck and not paralyzed. "How long ago?"

"The crash?" The guy shrugged. "Ten minutes?"

"Anybody else drive by?"

"Yeah, a white van. I think the side said Larson Construction. He slowed, asked me if I needed him to call 911, then drove off when I said I already did." He tugged on the folded-up door again.

"Let the fire department get me out. I appreciate your help. What's your name?"

"Cary Billings. I was headed home after my job at the burger place on Second Street. Good thing, huh?"

"Yeah. I'm Deputy Reynolds." Of course, if the

young man hadn't been on the road at that time, Rowan might've made it off the mountain without crashing. Man, his head hurt. He tried moving his left arm and gasped at the sharp pain that shot up his elbow. "Can you see my arm?"

"Yeah, it's cut pretty bad. You bleeding to death?"

Rowan chuckled. "I hope not."

Sirens wailed in the distance. "They're here." Cary waved his arms over his head.

The ambulance and fire truck stopped a few feet away, blocking the road. Two firemen rushed his way. "We'll have you out of there in no time."

As they pulled him out, Rowan endured the most excruciating pain he'd ever experienced. What had been numb came alive. A few times, he almost passed out especially when they lifted him onto the gurney. He reached out and grabbed the sleeve of one of the firemen. "Please call the sheriff and let him know that Deputy Reynolds has been in an accident and taken to Langley Hospital."

"Sure, buddy." He started to pat Rowan's shoulder, then thinking better of it, nodded. "I'll do that right now."

The paramedics took his vitals on the way to the hospital and wrapped the cut on his arm, then a nurse took his vitals again when he was rolled into a curtained room. She smiled. "I'll bring you something for the pain."

That's it? No clue as to how badly he was injured?

"How are you doing?" Sheriff Westbrook poked his head through the curtain. "I haven't seen the car yet, but you look pretty beat up."

"The car looks like an accordion." He raised the bed. "I haven't seen the doctor yet."

As if on cue, the doctor joined them. "Sorry about that. Busy night." He looked at the vitals on the computer screen. "Not too bad. How do you feel?" He shined a light in Rowan's eyes.

"Like I was in a car accident. Every part of me hurts."

The doctor chuckled. "You think you hurt today, wait until tomorrow. You've got a concussion, that's for sure." He checked Rowan's arm. "We'll stitch that. Anything else you're concerned about? We could do an x-ray."

Rowan gave himself a few minutes to see if any other part of him cried for attention. "My knees?"

The doctor rolled up his pants leg. "Swollen and bruised. I'm suggesting you lay low for a few days. I'll prescribe something for inflammation and pain. Come back if anything gets worse. The PA will be in to stitch you up in a minute."

"Guess you'll be out of the office for a few days." The sheriff plopped down in the vacant chair next to the bed.

"Have a mechanic look my car over, especially the brakes. I think it might've been tampered with."

The sheriff's eyes narrowed. "You serious?"

"Yep. Brakes acted funny. I think Larson wants me out of the picture, so don't have him look at the car."

The sheriff's face darkened. "Let's not assume anything without proof, but if your car was messed with, I'll haul him in for questioning. Enough is enough." He stood. "I'll check it out myself right now and get back to you."

"Sheriff?"

"Yeah?" He turned from the door.

"Could you let Shiloh know? She's watching Rachel for me. Oh, and Melinda Larson wouldn't say anything about who beat her."

Sheriff Westbrook shook his head. "I'll try asking her some questions, but I won't get to it until tomorrow. She'll be home by then. I'll send Deputy Hudson or Matchett here to give you a ride home."

"No need, sir. Shiloh can take me home." He knew without a doubt that she'd bring Rachel to see him.

The sheriff gave a nod and left Rowan to the PA's ministrations.

He sighed and laid his head back, hating that Rachel and Shiloh were alone. With him in the ER, they were vulnerable. They couldn't come see him fast enough.

~

Duke cursed and punched the door of his office at the garage. The deputy had to be one of the luckiest men alive. He should've died on that mountain.

Even worse was the fact that the Billings kid saw his van. Duke could've been working for someone. That might be a good reason he was there, but something easily checked.

Was Melinda home yet? She'd be his alibi if she was. He gave her a quick call.

"If anyone wants to know where I was all day, I was working on your barn. Got it? I came by today to do estimates. You home?"

"Got home earlier. Okay, Duke. I'll tell them." The woman sounded like a meek mouse. Where was her spirit? Why couldn't she be more like Shiloh?

"Good." He hung up and grabbed the keys to a sedan that had been brought it for repairs after it occurred to him that the deputy was at least temporarily out of the picture, which meant Shiloh was alone.

Duke parked out of sight of her house and peered around the corner of the Nelson house which gave him the perfect vantage point. He shrank back as the sheriff's car drove across the bridge and stopped in front of Shiloh's. Most likely he was there to tell her about Reynolds. That meant she'd be going to the hospital to see him. Which put her right in Duke's reach.

~

The doorbell rang, which set Peanut barking and scratching at the door. Shiloh peered through the peephole and froze at seeing Sheriff Westbrook on her porch. The man's grave expression told her he didn't come bearing good news.

Her hand trembled as she turned the knob and opened the door. "Sheriff?"

"Could you step out here, Miss Sloan? I'd rather the child not hear."

Her heart leaped into her throat. "Of course." She stepped out and closed the door behind her, but not before Peanut slipped out and sat at her feet, her dark eyes fixated on the sheriff.

He cut the dog a wary look. "Deputy Reynolds asked me to stop by and let you know he was involved in a car accident."

Her hand flew to her mouth. "Is he all right?"

"A bad cut on his arm, a concussion, lots of bruising, but he'll be good in a few days. He'd like you to watch Rachel until he gets home. He should be released later today, if you could pick him up."

"Can we go see him before he's released?" The thought of him lying in the hospital alone cut at her heart.

"I'm sure you can." He gave a nod and marched back to his car.

Shiloh would need to choose her words carefully so she didn't alarm Rachel. Taking a deep breath, she entered the house. "Rachel, come sit by me." She patted the sofa cushion.

"Okay." With a reluctant glance at the cartoon on the television, Rachel sat next to her.

Shiloh pressed off on the TV remote. "Everything will be okay. The sheriff said so, but your daddy was in a car wreck and is in the hospital. You'll be staying with me in the meantime. Would you like to go with me to bring him home?"

"Yes. Right now." Rachel stood. "He needs me."

"I'm sure he does." Shiloh grabbed her purse and car keys. "You have to stay here this time, Peanut." She set the alarm and followed Rachel to the car.

Rowan was sitting up in bed, his face already turning several shades of yellow and purple. His left arm had been bandaged. He grinned when they stepped into his alcove. "Just in time. I'm getting released with orders of a few days of rest."

"Rachel and I will make sure you follow the doctor's advice." Shiloh grinned, relieved he wasn't worse. If he were, the doctor wouldn't release him.

"You don't look good, Daddy." Rachel touched his

face, then the bandage on his arm.

"After I worked so hard on my makeup?" He raised his brows. "Give me a kiss. I'll feel better." He tapped his cheek.

"Not funny." She stood on tiptoe and gave him a kiss.

"Are you ready now?" Shiloh glanced at the papers in his lap.

"Yep. Waiting on a wheelchair." He raised a hand to stop her as she opened her mouth to speak. "Just a precaution because my knees are swollen."

"Okay." Shiloh would make sure he stayed at her house. She could take a few days off to take care of him. Between her and Rachel, they'd make him follow the doctor's orders. "We'll stop by your place to grab some things, then you two will stay with me."

"That isn't necessary."

"I insist. You've done so much for me; now let me do this for you. I'll pull the car next to the doors."

By the time she pulled up, the nurse had wheeled Rowan out, then helped him into the front seat. "Take care of yourself, Deputy." She tossed him a flirtatious smile, then wheeled the chair back into the building.

"Looks like you've made yourself an admirer." Despite her teasing, a trickle of jealousy ran through her.

"There's only one person whose admiration I want." He gave her hand a squeeze. "Let's go home."

She loved the sound of that coming from his lips. "I like that idea."

"Hmm." He closed his eyes and reclined his seat. "A catnap sounds good."

When she pulled from the parking lot, a dark sedan

pulled out behind her. As she merged into traffic heading for the exit ramp onto the Interstate, she noticed it was still there. After they passed two exits, she was sure they were being followed. She increased her speed, then shrugged off her silly notions. Why would someone follow her while a deputy was in the car?

As they drove, Rachel chattered on about all the ways she would help her father. Making him sandwiches, brushing his hair, reading him books…her list went on. Poor Rowan—her attention would wear him out.

She glanced in the rearview mirror again. The car had moved close enough that she could make out the figure of a man wearing a baseball cap. Duke? No. He didn't have a sedan. As far as she knew, all he had was the work van. If he did own a car, it would definitely be a newer model. The Larsons had always wanted people to know how great they were, even if they did work for a living like everyone else in town.

She glanced at Rowan and wondered whether she should wake him. He would know whether there was cause for concern.

As if sensing her thinking of him, he opened his eyes. "Did the sheriff tell you that I think my car was tampered with?"

"No." Her heart flew to her throat. "Are you sure?"

"They haven't checked it yet, but I'm pretty sure." He raised his seat, his voice groggy.

"Well, I think we're being followed."

Chapter Nineteen

Rowan moved his seat to an upright position and glanced out the back window. "Are you sure?"

"That car has been following us since we left the hospital."

His phone rang. It took some maneuvering to get it out of his pocket. "Reynolds."

"Your brake lines were cut. No doubt about it." The sheriff muttered something he didn't hear. "Where are you?"

"Headed down the Interstate toward my place. We're being followed, Sheriff. Mind sending some help? Mile marker 120 and headed west." He kept his gaze on the car behind them.

"Help is on the way." The sheriff hung up.

"Tighten your seatbelt, Rachel. Drive at a steady pace, Shiloh. Head for the sheriff's office."

"Do you think it's Duke? He doesn't own a car like that." Her knuckles whitened on the steering wheel.

"He owns a garage. He'd have his pick of any of the cars there to be worked on or sold." It definitely looked like Duke to him. Darn the pain meds that were making his brain fuzzy.

"You don't want me to try and outrun him?" Shiloh shot him a quick look.

"Absolutely not. I've already been in one accident today." He smiled at Rachel who had tears in her eyes. His brave little girl hadn't made a single whimper. "We'll be okay, sweetie."

"Promise?" Her chin quivered.

"Promise." He prayed it was a promise he could keep. How dare that man endanger his little girl.

"Daddy, are you spittin' mad?"

A sharp laugh escaped him. "You could say that."

Misty Mountain loomed to their right. He didn't relish a car chase on that mountain. Not after what he'd gone through that morning. Not with Rachel and Shiloh in the car.

Two sheriff department cars sped down the Interstate headed in the opposite direction. Good. Rowan had spotted a place where they could cross the median about a mile back.

"Help is coming."

Shiloh glanced in the rearview mirror. "Do you think he'll go away?"

"Who knows?" He shrugged. "But, at least we'll make it to our destination unscathed."

She gave him a shaky smile. "I'm going to hold you to that."

Deputy Hudson forced his car in between them and the man following them. Matchett took up the rear. Seconds later, the sedan veered off and sped through the median to head in the opposite direction.

"Promise kept." He exhaled heavily and slumped in his seat. "We still need to go to the sheriff's office.

I'll explain later." He put his head back and closed his eyes, secure in the fact they were safe. For now. At the office, he asked Shiloh to stay with Rachel and headed to speak to the sheriff.

Sheriff Westbrook glanced up from his desk when Rowan entered. "I thought you looked bad in the hospital. Shouldn't you be in bed?"

"Probably." He sat in a chair across from him. "Tell me about the cut brake line."

"Cleanly cut. I could tell for myself. No need for a mechanic. Could you ID the man following you?" He crossed his arms.

"Not one hundred percent, but I'm pretty sure it was Larson. Same build. Drove a navy Corolla, older model. Can we find out if he had that particular vehicle in the shop for repairs?"

"Shouldn't be too difficult. I'll send Matchett to the garage to look through his files." A serious expression settled on his face. "This is getting dangerous. If it is Larson, he'll go into hiding now and wait for his chance."

"Shiloh's house is the safest place around except for that renovated Victorian the mob boss used to own. No one can get in there."

"What if the electricity is cut off?"

"That's the only way. I'm hoping the dog would be enough warning to prevent that from happening." He'd have to do some thinking on how to keep that particular threat at bay. "Mind lending me your wife's dog, Shadow?" He grinned.

"She'd rather cut off my head." The sheriff laughed. "Those two are rarely parted. We could hire a couple of guard dogs. We have before. I'll also put out an APB on Larson. You staying at Miss Sloan's?"

"Yes. First, we're headed home to get a few things. I won't let her out of my sight. When I'm recovered, I'm going to hunt Larson down like a dog." He struggled to his feet with the speed of an old man. "Let me know about the dogs."

"They'll be there as soon as I can arrange it."

He joined his daughter and Shiloh in the reception area where Rachel munched on chips from the vending machine. "How about a burger?"

"We'll take it to go." Shiloh stood. "You need to be off your feet before you fall. You're swaying."

"I won't argue with you. These meds are kicking my butt." He wouldn't be taking them again because he needed his wits about him.

~

Duke hadn't thought about the deputy calling for help. What did the man think he would do with a child and a woman in the car?

He didn't hurt children, and unless Shiloh kept playing games, he wouldn't harm her. Now, he'd have to lay low. But, where? Melinda's place was his first choice. She'd never snitch on him. His cousin knew better. But, the sheriff's department was sure to look for him there.

Drumming his fingers on the steering wheel, Duke stared down the dirt road where he'd intended to ditch the vehicle. He needed an abandoned building that would still provide comfort. Roughing it was not his style. Laying low in any property owned by a Larson wouldn't work. Think, man!

It couldn't be too far away. He needed to be close enough to keep an eye on Shiloh so he didn't miss the opportunity to take her. He cursed the fact the deputy still lived. Having him dead would have solved a few problems. Now, Duke was back at square one, needing a new plan. Why couldn't it be easy to convince Shiloh of his feelings for her? All she needed to do was spend some time with him, then she'd see.

He scratched his head. There had to be a place in the woods behind her house. A hunter's cabin, a manufactured home, something.

He shoved the car door open and stepped onto the hard-packed surface of the road. Time to get moving. Once he found a place, he'd gather some supplies from the garage, and settle in. Then, he'd wait.

~

Shiloh listened in shock as Rowan filled her in on his brake lines. "You could've been killed."

"That was the intention." He slowly lowered onto a deck lounge. "I don't want Rachel to know."

"Of course not. I'm also taking a few days off work. It seems I'm needed here." She leaned against the railing and stared at the trees—a view that usually filled her with peace, but no more. The shadows looked threatening. The forest loomed like a giant beast waiting to devour her. She shook off her dark thoughts. "I'm going to clean up the wrappings from our burgers. Will you be okay out here?"

"Yep." He closed his eyes. "I'moing to take a little nap."

Tears stung her eyes as she cleaned up. Things were growing more dangerous with each passing day. If the other two deputies hadn't shown up today, who knew what would have happened on that highway? All she could think about as they drove was that if she could just reach the bridge, they'd be safe.

Were they? Someone tried to kill Rowan. Twice, it seemed, and she and Rachel would have died, too. She should never have come back to Misty Hollow.

Rachel moved past her and stared out the window in the back door. "Is Daddy sleeping?"

"Yes, sweetie. Let's not wake him, okay?" She forced a smile to her face.

"But…Sasquatch is back."

Shiloh's heart leaped into her throat as she rushed to the window as tires crunched gravel out front. Her gaze swept the woods behind the house. "I don't see anything."

"It was watching Daddy sleep. It's gone now."

The doorbell rang.

Peanut barked.

Shiloh kept her gaze on Rowan to see whether he'd wake. When he didn't, she ordered Rachel to hide in the pantry, then went to answer the door, grabbing a meat cleaver from the kitchen drawer on her way.

She peered through the peephole to see a middle-aged man in faded overalls standing on her porch. "Who is it?"

"Hank Owens, ma'am. The sheriff ordered some guard dogs to be delivered here."

Guard dogs? "I'm sorry, you must be—"

"He's right, Shiloh." Rowan stood next to her and eyed the cleaver. "Where's Rachel?"

"In the pantry. She saw Sasquatch again, outside, watching you. I thought…when the doorbell rang…"

"An intruder won't ring the doorbell. Put that down and come meet our hired four-legged friends. Rachel, come on out." He opened the door, looking better than he had all day.

"You should've told me." She set the cleaver on a small side table and joined him on the porch.

"Sorry." He opened the door and stepped outside. "Mr. Owens, I'm Deputy Reynolds." He offered his hand. "Thank you for coming."

"It's what I do." He whistled and two mastiffs bounded from the truck. "This is Tank and Butcher. They don't bark. They're more like the silent types, but they'll make sure no one sneaks up on you."

"Will they scare Sasquatch?" Rachel stared up at the man.

"Sasquatch? Well, I reckon they will." Mr. Owens grinned. "Not much scares these two."

"What about my dog? Will they be nice to her?" Shiloh patted the large heads.

"Sure. Bring her out."

She called for Peanut, who bounded outside, then stopped short at the sight of the two dogs. Her tail wagged slowly as she cut the other dogs a sideways glance. After much sniffing of behinds, they celebrated their new friendship by plopping in the dirt together.

"Good." She glanced at Rowan; there were so many questions, but she didn't want to say anything in front of the other man. Her questions would have to wait until Rachel was in bed. "Thank you, Mr. Owens. How long do we have these guys?"

"For as long as you need them. The sheriff's department is footing the bill." He tapped the brim of his hat, told the dogs to stay, then marched to his truck, whistling with every step.

Rowan sent Rachel into the house. With much pouting, she flounced inside declaring she wanted to stay outside and play with her new friends. When she'd closed the door, he turned to Shiloh. "I'm sorry I didn't tell you. The pain meds made me fuzzyheaded. When we stopped at the sheriff's office, he and I decided it might be a good idea to have these two here. It's been effective in the past on other cases."

She stared at his bruised face. "I trust your judgment. It took me by surprise is all. What do you think about Rachel seeing Sasquatch? She said it was watching you sleep."

"Creepy." He gave a lopsided grin. "It's most likely Larson. No more naps on the deck for any of us until this is over."

"If it's ever over." Her eyes traveled around the yard, then at the dogs. None of them seemed concerned.

"It will be. Trust me." He cupped her cheek. "I promise."

"Can you promise not to die on me?"

"I can promise to do my best not to." He gave her a quick kiss, then put his arm around her waist. "Let's go watch something silly on TV."

After a comedy that helped her forget the danger that lurked outside, even if only for ninety minutes, She made up the sofa as a bed for Rowan. Rachel would have the guest room.

As the others settled in, she let Peanut inside, then set the alarm and checked all the doors and windows. Rowan had offered, but after seeing the exhaustion coating his features, she declined. Her nightly routine helped give her a feeling of security.

She peered through the blinds on the back door and studied the shadows of the tree line. Nothing moved. No dogs raced for the trees. A full moon shone overhead, giving little room for anyone to hide—even Sasquatch. She exhaled heavily and headed for her room.

Chapter Twenty

After a week so uneventful even the dogs looked bored, Rowan announced he had a doctor's appointment that day hopefully to remove his stitches. "I shouldn't be gone more than a couple of hours."

Shiloh smiled over her shoulder from where she washed the breakfast dishes. "Rachel and I will spend that time making sure all her schoolwork is finished so she can go back on Monday when I do."

"Do I have to? I like doing my work here." Rachel frowned.

"I have a job to do and students waiting on me." She'd taken enough time off. Now that Rowan was pretty much healed, it was time to return to school.

Rowan gave her a kiss, snagged her keys from the table near the front door, and promised to bring back some burgers from the diner for lunch. "I'll be back as soon as I can."

Shiloh walked with him to the door, then set the alarm when he got in the car. Before returning to Misty Hollow, if someone would've told her that she'd have settled into a routine with a man, she'd have told them they were nuts. But, she'd fallen hard for a handsome deputy and his daughter. Her past no longer defined a future that looked bright for the first time in fifteen years.

She gathered up the throw rugs from the dryer and stepped onto the deck to hang them up. Tank and Butcher sprinted for the woods. It wasn't the first time, but the sight still left her uneasy.

"They're going after Sasquatch." Rachel appeared at her side as silent as a ghost.

"Have you seen him?"

She nodded.

"Why didn't you say something? I thought he'd gone away."

"Because it made you scared." She pressed against Shiloh. "He's always there watching."

"Let's go inside." She cast one more worried glance toward the trees, then ushered the child into the safety of the house. "Why don't you go watch a cartoon? The dogs can handle Sasquatch. Grab a cookie on your way."

The thought of a cookie seemed to have removed the flicker of fear from the little girl's face. "Yay. No more schoolwork."

Rachel's homework was at the bottom of her priorities. Keeping the child safe and distracted was number one. Shiloh returned to the house and locked the door.

Peanut stood at the front door, her nose pressed to the floor. She whined and pawed at the wood.

"The TV shut off," Rachel said.

Shiloh glanced at the microwave. Nothing. A study of the alarm system confirmed her fear. The electricity was off. She didn't recall a notice from the city saying it would be off for repairs. Which meant one thing.

Someone had shut it off.

The front door handle turned.

Peanut barked deep and loud.

"Rachel, come over here, please."

Eyes wide, she scooted off the sofa and came to Shiloh.

"When I say run, you grab my hand and we run as fast as we can out the back door, okay?" When the child nodded, Shiloh yanked open the door to the sight of Duke reaching for the handle again. "Get him, Peanut!"

The dog launched herself at him. Duke yelled then whipped around.

Grasping Rachel's hand, Shiloh darted out the back door and made for the woods as fast as possible. *Please, God, don't let him hurt my dog.* Shiloh knew exactly where to hide. Hopefully, Peanut could lead Rowan to them. She regretted not making the time to show him the cave. "You okay?" She took a quick glance at Rachel. "Can you keep up?"

"I can run fast. See?" She pulled free of Shiloh's grasp and sprinted ahead.

"Stay with me. You don't know the way." Shiloh turned to the right. "Time to get our feet wet."

Hopefully, they could hide their tracks by moving through the frigid water. The cold took her breath away, but she'd stashed new blankets for them in the cave.

It didn't take long for Rachel's lips to turn blue and her teeth to chatter. Please don't let her own impulsive decision make the child sick, Shiloh prayed. They splashed their way down creek a bit, then exited on the opposite side from where they'd entered.

She'd taken Peanut many times to the cave, mostly after an encounter with Duke. The dog should be able to find them if Duke didn't harm her.

"I'm tired." Rachel started to lag behind.

"We can't stop now. Soon." If they stopped, Duke would get them.

~

Duke grabbed a shovel from near the garage and swung it at the snarling dog. He hadn't had time to reach into his pocket for his gun.

The other two had been easy to take care of. A sleeping agent-soaked steak had done the trick. This one, though, wanted to tear his face off.

"Get back, you dirty scoundrel." He cursed, calling Shiloh the worst name he could think of. The woman had made her choice, and it wasn't him. So, he'd make her pay for how she'd ruined his life. With her and the deputy out of the picture, he could return to his everyday life. The town's residents would side with him as always.

The shovel connected, striking the dog in the ribcage. It yelped and fell back.

Without waiting to see how bad he'd hurt it, he dashed for the safety of the trees. Duke glanced back and noticed the open back door. He smiled. Shiloh and the kid had fled in the same direction he went. All he had to do now was track them before the two guard dogs woke up.

When he'd seen the deputy leave, he'd thought grabbing Shiloh would be easy without the alarm alerting her. The woman was smarter than he gave her credit for. Of course, she was. She was Shiloh. He wouldn't want her if she was stupid. He stopped just inside the tree line and listened. The kid wouldn't know to be quiet. On a chilly day like this one, she'd be whining. That's what kids did.

Duke couldn't hear anything but birds. He cursed the chattering cardinals that seemed to be taunting him. He studied the ground at his feet. Without rain for the last week, it didn't show prints. Where was she? He hadn't been sleeping in an abandoned trailer not to succeed in his quest to obtain her.

The child was a nuisance. He'd have to figure out what to do with her. He didn't like hurting animals or kids, but sometimes a man didn't have a choice.

Better yet, he'd use the kid as leverage to persuade the deputy to leave town. That would give Duke what he wanted. Shiloh.

~

Rowan grabbed the three burger meals from the passenger seat and headed for the front door. The whine of a dog pulled his attention to the side of the house.

"Peanut?" The dog lay under a rose bush. She belly crawled to him. "You okay?" Shiloh would be devastated if anything happened to her dog.

A skitter of fear ran up his spine. The dog didn't seem to be bleeding or have broken bones, but she trembled as if the devil himself was after her. The shovel lay in the middle of the yard. "Where're the girls? The other dogs? Did you put up a good fight?" He patted her head. "You're a good girl, aren't you?"

His mouth dried. His gut told him they weren't here, even before he checked the house. Rowan checked the fuse box, only to discover the wires were cut. When he spotted the open back door and didn't hear the wailing of the alarm, he knew his fears were founded. "Come on, Peanut. Let's find them."

Why hadn't he secured the box as he'd planned to?

Recovering from the accident had made him forget. He hadn't thought the danger great while he lived here. How wrong he was.

The dog perked up and trotted out the back door.

Rowan dropped the bags on the kitchen table, retrieved his gun from the painted pickle jar on top of the refrigerator, and followed. The fully-loaded gun was enough for what he needed.

Rachel's homework still sat on the coffee table. Rugs flapped in the wind on the back deck. Shiloh's phone sat on the counter. Things appeared as if Shiloh and Rachel would return at any moment. He made a quick call to the sheriff's department asking for backup, then ran toward the trees.

"Find them, Peanut."

The dog barked and, nose to the ground, headed south. Rowan followed.

He wasn't much of a praying man, but he prayed more as he searched for Shiloh and his daughter than he had since Rose was diagnosed with cancer. Her life hadn't been spared, but she had lived longer than the doctors gave her. It had been something.

Now that he was ready to love again, he didn't want a repeat of losing the woman he loved. He had to find her and his daughter. Then, he'd hunt Duke down like the rat he was.

Peanut led him to the guard dogs. Steak bones lay next to them. They both were breathing. At least the man wasn't into killing animals. After making sure they were okay, Rowan let them be and coaxed Peanut to continue.

She took one last look at them, whined in her throat, and headed down the creek.

Shiloh had mentioned a place special to her once. She'd even promised to take him there. Hopefully, that's where she and Rachel hid. Hopefully, he'd have the chance to spend time there with her.

Chapter Twenty-One

"Up there." Shiloh pointed for Rachel to start climbing. "Hurry. We can't let Duke find us."

The child scampered up like a monkey, then stared back at Shiloh.

"Here." She parted the brush hiding the cave's entrance.

"No way. It's dark in there."

"I have a light. Go." She gave her a small shove.

The darkness inside the cave engulfed them. "Sit against the wall while I cover the entrance. Then, I'll light the lantern." Her fingers were numb from splashing through the creek, her feet, soaked and aching.

Once the brush was back in place, she crawled to where Rachel huddled. Finding the blankets, she handed the child one and wrapped another around her shoulders before finding the lantern. Minutes later, a small flame cut through the inky blackness.

Shiloh removed Rachel's shoes and socks, then her own, and tucked them under the blanket. "We have to be quiet. I have some granola bars and water in that backpack. If you have to go to the bathroom, use the far corner. I don't know how long we'll be here." *Please,*

God, not long.

Shiloh pulled Rachel close so they could share each other's warmth. "This used to be my special place," she whispered. "My parents fought a lot. They weren't as nice as your father, so I would come here and pretend this was my home. A place that belonged just to me. I still come here sometimes when I want to be alone."

"But you live alone." She rested her head on Shiloh's shoulder.

"I know. Silly, isn't it?"

She shrugged. "When we first got here, I thought this was where Sasquatch lived."

"There's no such thing."

"Well, something was out there."

Shiloh exhaled long and slow. "Yes, but it's just a man. A very bad man." One she prayed wouldn't find them. They had nowhere to go if he stepped into the cave.

"It's okay. Daddy arrests bad guys. He'll save us."

"Of course, he will." Shiloh tightened her arm around the child. "Why not take a little nap? Maybe by the time you wake up, your father will be here."

"Okay." Rachel rolled into the blanket as if it were a cocoon and curled up next to the lantern.

Sleep did sound good after their flight through the woods. Shiloh's eyes drifted closed.

A twig snapped outside. Her eyes popped open. She put her hand over Rachel's mouth when she bolted to an upright position.

Shiloh grinned at Rachel as a squirrel scampered inside, but her relief was short-lived. The ensuing rustling of leaves alerted her to the fact it hadn't been the squirrel that made the noise that woke her.

Rachel whimpered.

"Shh." Shiloh turned off the lantern, pitching them back into darkness. She scooted Rachel further from the entrance and pulled her onto her lap.

Shiloh's heartbeat so loud she was certain whoever or whatever was out there could hear. She willed her heart rate to slow and fought to control her breathing when everything in her wanted to dart from the cave and flee.

A scream almost escaped her as something charged into the cave. A wet tongue made her laugh. She wrapped her arms around Peanut's neck. "I knew you'd find us. Where's Rowan, huh? Did you ditch him, or is he not back from the doctor's yet?"

She felt a hundred times better with the dog there. Peanut would alert them if Duke came. Maybe even scare the man off. If not, he'd help Shiloh fightg. She knew without a doubt that her dog would defend her when necessary. That had been proven earlier when Duke arrived.

The dog whined as she wrapped her arm around her. More gently, she ran her hands up and down the dog's ribcage. Her skin rippled. A small bump rose under the skin. Duke had hurt her! "My poor baby." She laid her head against the dog's. "We'll see that he pays, baby. You wait and see."

Rachel scooted between Shiloh and Peanut. "I feel better with her here. She can bite the bad guy."

Shiloh contemplated turning the lantern back on but decided against it. Since Rachel didn't scem as frightened of the dark with the dog here, she thought it best they stay in the dark.

How would Rowan find them without Peanut to guide him? She needed to leave and search for him. Rachel would be fine with Peanut. It was Shiloh Duke was after. Not the little girl.

"I'm going to go look for your father. Peanut will watch over you." She got to her feet.

"No, please." Rachel tugged at the hem of her shirt. "You can't leave us."

"I have to. Your father won't be able to find us in here."

"Then take us with you." Rachel stood. "If you don't, I'll follow you. I might get lost. It'll be all your fault."

The little imp. Shiloh sighed. "Okay, but you do exactly what I tell you when I tell you. Got it?"

"Yes."

She could hear the satisfied grin in the child's answer. It couldn't be helped. She knew Rachel enough to know that she would do exactly as she said. Shiloh didn't worry about her getting lost—not with Peanut—but there were other dangers in the woods.

They snuck from the cave and entered dusk. The sun had begun its descent, and it fell faster among the trees.

Shiloh gripped Rachel's hand. "Find Rowan, Peanut."

The dog woofed and headed away from the cave.

Shiloh and Rachel followed, sliding more than climbing, until they reached the bottom. Still wearing the blankets around their shoulders, she found the trek more comfortable. Still, an uneasiness settled deep into her bones. *Rowan, where are you?*

~

Peanut bounding off had been unexpected. Now, Rowan was searching unfamiliar territory. Shiloh and Rachel, if Duke hadn't already nabbed them, could be anywhere. It didn't help that night was falling and it would be dark in half an hour.

Shiloh, where are you? Where is my backup?

Rachel screamed in the distance.

A dog barked.

Peanut had found them. But where?

Rowan turned in a circle, trying to pinpoint where the scream had come from. Another scream. He darted toward the creek he'd left behind and followed it as fast as he could. He burst into a clearing and skidded on the dry leaves.

Larson held Rachel close to him and aimed a gun at her head. Tears streamed down her pale face.

"Daddy!" Her cry wrenched his heart.

Shiloh held tight to a frenzied Peanut's collar. She turned wide eyes on him, relief flooding her features at the sight of him.

Heart beating in his throat, Rowan aimed his weapon at Larson. "Let her go."

"Not unless you give me something." His eyes flashed. "You shoot me; I shoot her. Not even you are a good enough shot to drop me from that distance. Lower your gun."

What he said was true. Rowan lowered his weapon. "What do you want?"

"For you to take your daughter and leave Misty Hollow. Then, Shiloh can focus on me and realize how much she means to me. We can't be together while you're around." He shrugged. "Since you refuse to die, I'll have to send you away."

The man was certifiable insane. "I can't just pick up and go, Larson. I have a commitment to this city."

"You aren't a native. Nobody will care." His hold on Rachel tightened, eliciting a yelp from her.

"You're hurting her." Rowan took a step forward.

"Don't come any closer. Shiloh, you're losing the battle with that dog. If you release her, she'll die. I won't fail this time to stop the beast."

"Let Rachel go, Duke. I'll come willingly with you if you let Rowan and his daughter walk away. I'll come now." Her eyes shimmered in the moonlight. "Please. If you hurt them, I can never love you. Surely, you understand."

Confusion crossed his face. He glanced from her to Rowan, then back again. "You're messing with my head. You've loved me since prom night."

"I've hated you since that night. If you have any chance of being with me, you must let them go."

"No." His eyes narrowed as his head shook side to side. "You're trying to hurt me with your words."

She dragged Peanut to Rowan. "Hold her."

"What are you doing?"

"Trading places with Rachel." Her gaze softened. "I have to. Then, you can take her and go."

"I'm not leaving you with him." He couldn't, not knowing what he'd do to her. At first, he'd be kind, but after that she'd end up like Melinda, broken and bruised.

"You have to." She turned and inched toward Larson.

He grinned. "I knew you'd come to your sense." He shoved Rachel to the side, causing her to stumble.

"Hold it." Sheriff Westbrook and Deputy Matchett

stepped into the clearing. "Drop the gun, Larson."

As he reached for Shiloh, the sheriff fired. The first shot took him in the left shoulder, spinning him. When he raised his right hand to fire, Matchett's shot took him down.

Rachel leaped into Rowan's arms.

Peanut's barking increased.

Shiloh sagged to the ground.

"Come on, baby." He took Rachel and knelt next to Shiloh. "It's over, sweetheart. It's finally over." He wrapped both his arms around his girls. "Can I take them home, Sheriff?"

"Yes. I'll stop by tomorrow to get your stories."

Rowan helped Shiloh to her feet and headed to the home he never intended to leave.

Epilogue

Six months later.

Rowan and Shiloh sat on the back deck and watched Rachel and Peanut play. He reached over and took her hand. "How does it feel to be Mrs. Reynolds for five months now?"

"Old hat." She laughed. "I'm glad you decided to live here. I've come to love this house."

"I know how much it means to you."

She nodded. All the work she'd put into the property had erased the bad memories. Now, with a husband and stepdaughter, she'd make new ones with them. "I have something to tell you."

"I wondered what secret lurked in those beautiful eyes. Does it have something to do with the phone call you received earlier?" He tilted his head.

"Yes." Butterflies danced in her stomach. "How do you feel about being a father again?"

"What?" He jumped to his feet, knocking over the glass of tea on the side table. "Really?"

She nodded as he pulled her up. "The doctor confirmed it."

He cupped her face and kissed her. "That's the best

news I've heard since you agreed to marry me."

"You're okay with it? I mean, Rachel is eight and—"

"Will be ecstatic when she hears she's going to be a big sister. Oh, Shiloh. I do love you." He wrapped her in a hug.

"How much?" She giggled, laying her head against his chest.

"More than words can ever express."

She sighed. Coming home to Misty Hollow had been the best decision she could ever have made. It hadn't been easy, far from it, but she'd persevered, rebuilt, and found a new family. Rowan was everything her father and Duke hadn't been. She finally felt cherished and didn't want to be anywhere else.

Thank you, Misty Hollow, for welcoming me back.

The End

Dear Reader,

Thank you for spending more time in Misty Hollow. If you enjoyed Bridge to Safety, please head to Amazon and consider leaving a review. Reviews are very important to an author and helps other readers discover their books.

God Bless!

Cynthia Hickey

www.cynthiahickey.com

Cynthia Hickey is a multi-published and best-selling author of cozy mysteries and romantic suspense. She has taught writing at many conferences and small writing retreats. She and her husband run the publishing press, Winged Publications. They live in Arizona and Arkansas, becoming snowbirds with three dogs. They have ten grandchildren who keep them busy and tell everyone they know that "Nana is a writer."

    Connect with me on FaceBook
    Twitter
    Sign up for my newsletter and receive a free short story
    www.cynthiahickey.com

    Follow me on Amazon
    And Bookbub
  Shop my bookstore on shopify. For better price and autographed.

Enjoy other books by Cynthia Hickey

Misty Hollow
Secrets of Misty Hollow

Deceptive Peace
Calm Surface
Lightning Never Strikes Twice
Lethal Inheritance
Bitter Isolation
Say I Don't
Christmas Stalker
Bridge to Safety

Stay in Misty Hollow for a while. Get the entire series here!

The Seven Deadly Sins series
Deadly Pride
Deadly Covet
Deadly Lust
Deadly Glutton
Deadly Envy
Deadly Sloth
Deadly Anger

The Tail Waggin' Mysteries
Cat-Eyed Witness
The Dog Who Found a Body
Troublesome Twosome
Four-Legged Suspect
Unwanted Christmas Guest
Wedding Day Cat Burglar

Brothers Steele

BRIDGE TO SAFETY

Sharp as Steele
Carved in Steele
Forged in Steele
Brothers Steele (All three in one)

The Brothers of Copper Pass
Wyatt's Warrant
Dirk's Defense
Stetson's Secret
Houston's Hope
Dallas's Dare
Seth's Sacrifice
Malcolm's Misunderstanding
The Brothers of Copper Pass Boxed Set

Time Travel
The Portal

Tiny House Mysteries
No Small Caper
Caper Goes Missing
Caper Finds a Clue
Caper's Dark Adventure
A Strange Game for Caper
Caper Steals Christmas
Caper Finds a Treasure
Tiny House Mysteries boxed set

Wife for Hire – Private Investigators

CYNTHIA HICKEY

Saving Sarah
Lesson for Lacey
Mission for Meghan
Long Way for Lainie
Aimed at Amy
Wife for Hire (all five in one)

A Hollywood Murder
Killer Pose, book 1
Killer Snapshot, book 2
Shoot to Kill, book 3
Kodak Kill Shot, book 4
To Snap a Killer
Hollywood Murder Mysteries

Shady Acres Mysteries
Beware the Orchids, book 1
Path to Nowhere
Poison Foliage
Poinsettia Madness
Deadly Greenhouse Gases
Vine Entrapment
Shady Acres Boxed Set

CLEAN BUT GRITTY Romantic Suspense

Highland Springs

Murder Live
Say Bye to Mommy

BRIDGE TO SAFETY

To Breathe Again
Highland Springs Murders (all 3 in one)

Colors of Evil Series

Shades of Crimson
Coral Shadows

The Pretty Must Die Series

Ripped in Red, book 1
Pierced in Pink, book 2
Wounded in White, book 3
Worthy, The Complete Story

Lisa Paxton Mystery Series

Eenie Meenie Miny Mo
Jack Be Nimble
Hickory Dickory Dock
Boxed Set

Hearts of Courage
A Heart of Valor
The Game
Suspicious Minds
After the Storm
Local Betrayal
Hearts of Courage Boxed Set

Overcoming Evil series
Mistaken Assassin
Captured Innocence
Mountain of Fear
Exposure at Sea
A Secret to Die for
Collision Course
Romantic Suspense of 5 books in 1

INSPIRATIONAL

Nosy Neighbor Series
Anything For A Mystery, Book 1
A Killer Plot, Book 2
Skin Care Can Be Murder, Book 3
Death By Baking, Book 4
Jogging Is Bad For Your Health, Book 5
Poison Bubbles, Book 6
A Good Party Can Kill You, Book 7
Nosy Neighbor collection

Christmas with Stormi Nelson

The Summer Meadows Series
Fudge-Laced Felonies, Book 1
Candy-Coated Secrets, Book 2
Chocolate-Covered Crime, Book 3
Maui Macadamia Madness, Book 4
All four novels in one collection

The River Valley Mystery Series
Deadly Neighbors, Book 1
Advance Notice, Book 2
The Librarian's Last Chapter, Book 3
All three novels in one collection

Historical cozy
Hazel's Quest

Historical Romances
Runaway Sue
Taming the Sheriff
Sweet Apple Blossom
A Doctor's Agreement
A Lady Maid's Honor
A Touch of Sugar
Love Over Par
Heart of the Emerald
A Sketch of Gold
Her Lonely Heart

Finding Love the Harvey Girl Way
Cooking With Love
Guiding With Love
Serving With Love
Warring With Love
All 4 in 1

Finding Love in Disaster
The Rancher's Dilemma
The Teacher's Rescue
The Soldier's Redemption

Woman of courage Series

A Love For Delicious
Ruth's Redemption
Charity's Gold Rush
Mountain Redemption
They Call Her Mrs. Sheriff
Woman of Courage series

Short Story Westerns
Flowers of the Desert

Contemporary

Romance in Paradise
Maui Magic
Sunset Kisses
Deep Sea Love
3 in 1

Finding a Way Home
Service of Love
Hillbilly Cinderella

BRIDGE TO SAFETY

Unraveling Love
I'd Rather Kiss My Horse

Christmas
Dear Jillian
Romancing the Fabulous Cooper Brothers
Handcarved Christmas
The Payback Bride
Curtain Calls and Christmas Wishes
Christmas Gold
A Christmas Stamp
Snowflake Kisses
Merry's Secret Santa
A Christmas Deception

The Red Hat's Club (Contemporary novellas)

Finally
Suddenly
Surprisingly
The Red Hat's Club 3 – in 1

Short Story

One Hour (A short story thriller)
Whisper Sweet Nothings (a Valentine short romance)

Made in the USA
Monee, IL
05 May 2023